Hanging Around in the Pyrenees

Hanging Around in the Pyrenees

Elly Grant

Books by the Author

Death in the Pyrenees series:

- Palm Trees in the Pyrenees

- Grass Grows in the Pyrenees

- Red Light in the Pyrenees

- Dead End in the Pyrenees

- Deadly Degrees in the Pyrenees

- Hanging Around in the Pyrenees

Angela Murphy series:

- The Unravelling of Thomas Malone

- The Coming of the Lord

Also by Elly Grant

- Never Ever Leave Me

- Death at Presley Park

- But Billy Can't Fly

- Twists and Turns

Hanging around

Everything looked strange to the man as he stumbled towards the trees. His head felt woolly and the ground beneath his feet seemed cushioned, as if he was walking on cotton wool. The man was unsure of where he was, or for that matter, where he'd been. He hadn't drunk much alcohol but the pills he'd ingested were undoubtedly the cause of his confusion. The landscape looked as if it were melting, stretching and bending surreally, like a Dali painting. The ladder in front of him was leaning against a sweet chestnut tree, its rungs and sides twisted and rippled like snakes writhing. The nut cases attached to the branches of the tree, were spiky like hedgehogs and, as he tried to focus on them, he believed they were hedgehogs, so he was extra careful not to touch their spines. Under the influence of the mind-altering drugs, they'd become alive to him, and he wondered how the creatures had managed to climb up the steep trunk of the tree.

The man gripped the sides of the ladder and with faltering steps, he began to ascend. The voice in his head kept talking, instructing him, and he felt compelled to obey. On reaching the top of the ladder he eyed the loop of stout rope which hung from a thick branch and reached out for it. He liked the feel of the noose in his hands. It reminded him of a braid of hair. He rubbed it gently against his cheek imagining it belonged to a beautiful girl. In this dreamlike state the beautiful girl wanted him to caress her, he could picture her willowy frame, feel her skin, smell her perfume. He inhaled deeply and felt a familiar stirring in his loins. Now he could hear her voice urging him on, telling him what to do. Carefully, he drew the noose over his head and tightened it around his neck, wobbling slightly on the ladder from the exertion. Then he looked up, marvelling at the myriad of sparkling diamonds dancing across the black, night sky. The voice in his head kept talking, but he could no longer concentrate, he was tired now and he just wanted to lie down on his bed and go to sleep.

For a split second the world stood still then he tumbled, dropping, before a sudden, sickening jolt halted his fall. The last thing he heard was a loud crack as his neck broke. Then, the only sounds in the night were from the cicadas, rubbing their legs together in a macabre applause, and the creak of the trees in the cool night breeze.

Chapter 1

I am sitting at the table and the sun is streaming in through the open door. Even though it's near the end of October, the light is bright and sharp. There is no chill in the air, the temperature is still over twenty degrees, but my garden shows signs of autumn. Ollee, my dog, lies at my feet, his head resting on his paws. He's not asleep, his eyes are open, and his bat-like ears are twitching. He sighs as he watches me put the last bite of my croissant into my mouth. The open pot of blackberry jelly seems to be winking at me, tempting me to eat more of the delicious preserve and, as I reach for some warm baguette, Ollee sits up and licks his lips expectantly, his eyes never leaving mine.

"That dog has had quite enough to eat this morning," my friend Patricia says. She shakes her finger at Ollee who lies back down. "He stole some cheese out of the shopping bag. I left the packet on the floor while I unpacked the rest of the groceries. Little thief," she admonishes.

Ollee has the good sense to look guilty. He sighs once more before standing and slinking off into the garden.

"I'm so relieved that my fruit and nuts have now been harvested and dealt with," Patricia says. "Your Papa was wonderful. I'd never have coped without him. My orchard has produced so much this year, it's amazing. Now that the nuts and apples are stored, I'm free to get on with my paintings for the Christmas sales."

Patricia's face is bright and happy. For those of you who haven't met us before, we are best friends, like sisters, in fact. We live in our lovely house in the foothills of the eastern Pyrenees with Ollee our dog and Mimi our cat. We also have several hens and some rabbits, but their numbers change from time to time depending on what is being cooked for dinner. I am the most senior police person in the area having risen from near obscurity in a very short time, helped by the deaths of some very unsavoury characters. Solving major crimes propelled me forward to the highly esteemed position I now enjoy. Patricia and I are well respected in town and many important people want to socialise with us, although some wagging tongues still try to imply we are more than just friends. They cannot accept us living together because Patricia is a lesbian who doesn't hide her inclinations. I love Patricia and I would do anything for her, and she loves me, but we are not lovers. We are in our late thirties and she too has come from nothing, but she now has her own business producing pies and preserves. The demand for her produce far outstrips the amount she can supply so next year we are going to look for a local, professional kitchen to rent and an employee or two to work for her. Patricia is very talented and is also well known as an artist. I am so proud of her achievements.

"Danielle, Danielle, you're daydreaming. I asked you what you'd like to do today." Patricia's words cut through my thoughts.

"I'd prefer not to be in town on my day off, but apart from that, anything you like."

Her blue eyes sparkle. "You'll think I'm mad after the amount of work I've done gathering in my crop, but I'd like to go into the mountains to find chestnuts. I've been given this great recipe for making something the English call stuffing. It's made from apricots and chestnuts and you can freeze it. Chestnuts don't keep the way other nuts do. So, they can't be stored, but they can be cooked and frozen."

"You're right. I do think you're mad to give yourself more work. But it's a glorious day and there'll be no problem finding them; besides I'll get to eat the produce, so I won't complain. Ollee will enjoy the outing. You fetch some baskets and I'll get the car ready."

Within a few minutes we are on our way heading for the nearby town of Ceret. I pick my way up the narrow winding road behind the town. On one side, great, jagged rocks poke out from the mountainside, and on the other the land falls steeply away. The drop seems bottomless. For some reason the occasional cars coming down the mountain towards us are travelling very fast. I am forced to stop as we attempt to manoeuvre around one another, without one car being scraped on the rocks or the other plummeting down the mountainside.

"I don't understand why these stupid people are going so fast," Patricia says nervously. She is gripping the edges of her seat. "Are they trying to cause an accident?"

"Don't worry. A couple of more minutes and we'll be stopping. I know a good place where we can pull off the road," I reply, trying to reassure her.

When I do pull in, she releases her bated breath and I too am relieved. I'd forgotten how horrible the drive was, although the scenery is breath taking. We are over five hundred metres up and the view is spectacular. The mountain seems to flatten out at this point and fields of trees stretch out on both sides of the road. Most are fenced with electric fencing to protect the crops from wild boar and the occasional human raider, but chestnut trees are everywhere, and the nuts and prickly shells cover the road and verges.

"This is perfect," Patricia says delightedly.

As she opens the car door, Ollee jumps from the back seat to the front, and using Patricia as a spring board, pushes past her and leaps out. At least the exuberant dog understands about roads I think, and I'm pleased to see that as he runs off, he avoids stepping on the tarmac.

We are like children again as we pick up the rich, brown nuts, and even though they will all taste the same when cooked, the delight of finding larger specimens thrills us. A myriad of butterflies, in every colour, flutter round us, and every so often we hear the sound of rustling as nuts fall from the trees and the crack as they hit the ground. The noise startles Ollee and he barks and jumps around, looking first skywards and then at the ground. His confusion is hilarious, and we laugh every time he does this.

"What is it, Ollee? Is it a rabbit?" Patricia says, as another nut hits the ground. "There it is," she says pointing, and the dog takes off barking, looking for the creature he assumes made the sound.

"At the rate the nuts are falling, it should keep him amused for ages," I say. "How many kilos do you want?"

"I can use whatever we gather because once they're cooked and out of the shell they won't take up too much room in the freezer. But there'll be plenty available as they're still falling, so don't knock yourself out. It's surprisingly hot today for working."

We continue collecting for a while longer, then I take two folding chairs from the car and we sit in the sun and relax, inhaling the perfumed air and listening to Ollee's intermittent barking.

"This is idyllic," Patricia says. "How lucky we are to live in this region."

"We are very lucky," I agree.

Our rest is disturbed by Ollee's barking when we realise it has become persistent.

"What's the matter with that dog now?" Patricia asks.

"I hope he hasn't cornered a wild boar. There are lots of them here in the mountains. We'd better check."

I look around and pick up a sturdy stick for protection, just in case, and we follow the sound of his barking. We cut through some trees and see Ollee jumping around near a clearing. He is looking skyward and barking excitedly.

"Not a boar, thank goodness," Patricia says. "More likely a bird or a squirrel."

Our attention is on the dog, and at first, we see nothing else. We continue to walk forward for a better look. A breeze blows and there is a loud creaking sound. We both look up. Patricia's hand shoots to her mouth. "Oh, mon Dieu," she whispers.

We are startled. There is a body hanging from the tree. It's a man. A stout rope is tightly wound around his neck and he's dressed smartly in a white shirt and beige trousers. His brown shoes are highly polished. His clothes are more suited to an office than this rural spot and he looks out of place in this setting.

"Suicide," I mutter. "I'd better phone for help."

"How did he get up there?" Patricia asks.

I look around. "There, in the long grass," I say pointing. "There's a ladder. He must have climbed up the tree then kicked it away."

"His hands are purple where the blood has gathered, but he doesn't seem to have been here long. The vultures haven't pecked out his eyes yet," Patricia says matter-of-factly.

She is rather an expert on corpses as she worked for many years in the local funeral parlour. The man's eyes are staring blankly; his face is contorted, and his head is at an angle with his neck clearly broken. It's difficult to determine his age, but not young. His body is fat and his hair, such as there is of it, is grey. The man's trousers are discoloured from the bodily fluids which he evacuated during death. The faecal smell cuts through the gentle aniseed perfume of the surrounding wild fennel.

"What a lonely way to end your life, but at least the setting is beautiful," I observe.

"I shouldn't have said the day was idyllic," Patricia replies. "I should have known it was tempting fate."

Chapter 2

We return to our chairs. There is no point in standing around waiting for the emergency services to arrive or for the corpse to decompose and stink further. After some time, a car arrives from Ceret with two young police officers inside, then a couple of minutes later, a fire service vehicle. I am disappointed that my friend, Jean, is not one of the pompiers on the truck.

"Does anyone recognise the hanged man?" I ask. I am met with blank stares.

"I don't think he lives locally or one of us would surely know him," a fireman says, and we all nod in agreement.

Another vehicle approaches. Inside is my assistant Paul. He joins us.

"Poullet is on his way. Pierre Junot is driving him. You might want to put on your lipstick, Boss," he adds, making a joke.

"How on earth did Junot hear about this?" I ask. "The last thing I want is that idiot snapping away with his camera and making stupid assumptions."

Pierre Junot is our local photographer and sometimes he works as a freelance journalist.

"Doctor Poullet's car is in the garage. Remember it failed its CT because all the tyres were bald, and the emissions were poisonous. Junot is his neighbour," Paul explains.

"Merde," I reply. "Why didn't you drive the old fool?"

"I tried, Boss, but he said Junot's car is bigger and more comfortable."

"He should go on a diet," I reply bitterly. "He's the size of a baby elephant. With all of us hanging around, this is becoming a circus."

Eventually, an old battered Peugot comes into view. It is backfiring and coughing its way along the track. It splutters and jumps before stopping behind the fire truck. Junot leaps out, his camera swinging from a strap around his neck.

"If he gets in my way I'll suspend him from that and hang him next to the corpse," I hiss, and Paul laughs.

The passenger door is thrown open. "Junot, Junot, get me out of this contraption," the unmistakeable voice of Doctor Poullet calls. It takes Junot and a laughing Paul a few moments to extricate his enormous bulk from the car. The doctor mops at his sweaty face with a damp, limp handkerchief. "Well, where is the unfortunate man? Are we going to stand around all day? Has someone brought a picnic? Maybe we'll play petanque," he scowls.

"This way my friend," I reply, pointing the way.

"Do we know who he is?" Poullet asks.

"Nobody recognises him, but perhaps you or Junot will enlighten us," I reply.

Once again, we all stand around observing the corpse which is gently swinging in the breeze.

Poullet sighs audibly and mops his brow again. "His name is Henri Boudin. He is sixty-four years of age and yesterday evening he dined on a very fine cassoulet. He used to live in Ceret, but now he resides in Argeles."

"You can tell all that just by looking at the corpse hanging there?" Junot asks incredulously.

"No, you idiot," Poullet replies, "I can tell you this because he is my wife's cousin and he dined with us last night."

We are shocked. All of us stand in stunned silence uncomfortable that one of our numbers is connected to a suicide. It is as if Poullet has let off a fart. We are embarrassed for him, but don't know how to move on. After a moment, he says, "I'm feeling a bit faint. I must sit down." The awkwardness is broken, and we rally to assist him.

"Here, Doctor, sit down here," Junot says, and I'm pleased to see him indicating towards a wide tree stump and not one of my folding chairs which would never hold Poullet's bulk.

Junot begins to snap away with his camera.

"Have you no compassion?" Paul says shortly. "Our friend has just lost his cousin."

"My wife's cousin," Poullet corrects. "I hardly knew the man and I'd never really taken to him; we had nothing in common. But one thing is certain, he was not suicidal when I was with him last night. Something doesn't add up."

"Perhaps the Doc's company was simply too much to bear," one of the cops from Ceret mutters, cracking a joke with his colleague to lighten the mood.

"I'm commandeering your photos, Junot," I instruct. This might not be all it seems. We could be standing in a crime scene.

"What should we do about the body?" a fireman asks. "Should we lift him down? We can't leave him hanging there in the sun or he'll turn into a kebab."

All eyes are on the doctor.

"Yes, yes, cut him down. I think you'll learn more from asking me questions and from the autopsy. There's no reason to keep him hanging around. You'd better ask Doctor Picard to do the post mortem as I'm connected to Henri, and for all you know, I could have murdered the man."

"But you didn't kill him Doctor, did you?" Paul asks the direct question that somehow has become stuck in my throat.

"No, I did not, and before you ask, neither did my wife's cooking."

I arrange for Paul to take Patricia and Ollee home, so I can concentrate on the job in hand. So much for having a day off, I think. Then I spend the next hour taking notes.

"Where is Henri's car?" Poullet asks. "Has someone driven it back to town?"

"What car?" I ask aloud. "I haven't seen a car."

"So, you thought he walked halfway up a mountain, at night, carrying a ladder?" Poullet says, and he raises his eyebrows at me. "And I thought you were clever, Danielle. Where did he get the ladder? Do people just leave random ladders lying around? Isn't that usual?" He and Junot exchange smirks and I feel my face redden.

"I have many questions which need to be answered," I reply. "There would be no reason for the police to investigate if all crimes came solved and neatly packaged. Besides, there is still the chance Henri killed himself."

"Not likely," Poullet replies stubbornly.

"Not likely," Junot agrees.

I scowl at Junot. "Go home," I say. "You're finished here."

"But perhaps...," he begins.

"Perhaps nothing," I say. "Go home and take the doctor with you. He's had a bad shock," I add, leaving him no excuse to remain.

"I would like to leave now, Monsieur Junot, please. We can talk in the car. I still have to inform my poor wife about her cousin."

"Of course, Doctor. Right away, Doctor. Let me open the car door for you, Doctor. We can indeed talk in the car." He flashes me a triumphant smile and I'm so annoyed I could slap him.

"This is an ongoing case," I say, as Poullet throws himself into the passenger seat rocking the car alarmingly. "You must not discuss it with anyone."

Junot slams the door shut then goes around to the driver's side and climbs in.

"Yeah, right," he answers then he starts the engine and pulls away in a cloud of exhaust fumes.

"Bastard," I say, and I bang my clenched fist on my forehead with frustration.

After I gather the information I require, I leave the junior officers to finish things off at the scene then I telephone Paul and arrange to meet him in the office. We will have to formally interview Doctor and Madame Poullet, a task I'm dreading. He'll need the words dragged from his lips and she will never shut up. Neither will be able to tell us much, I suspect. Then I call Patricia to make sure she got home, and she answers on the third ring.

"Is that you finished now, Danielle? Are you on your way home?"

When I explain that I must go into work, I can hear the disappointment in her voice, but she knows my hands are tied and there's nothing I can do.

"Don't worry about us," she replies. "Ollee and I will go for a walk then I'll cook something special for dinner. I'll open a bottle of good red wine to let it breathe. At least we'll be able to relax in the garden when you do return. After this month ends and things become quieter you'll be able to take most Saturdays off."

She's right, of course; things do wind down in November. And in December, when Le Therme, the spa, closes for the winter and all the 'curists' go home, the town too seems to shut down.

As I drive back, I try to formulate in my head the questions I need answered. I also find myself staring into fields and lanes in case I see Henri Boudin's car. Poullet said it was a blue Renault estate with a roof rack and a tow bar. He also told me it had bumps the length of the passenger side where Henri had an accident with a gate post while parking, so it shouldn't be too difficult to identify. If Henri drove himself to the field and his car is gone then the person who drove it away is involved in his death. But why he was killed, and who this person is, is a complete mystery to me.

Chapter 3

When I meet with Paul at the office we decide to leave the interviews with Poullet and his wife until Monday. Neither of us can face them today, and besides, it probably won't make any difference to the information we receive.

"Hopefully Madame Poullet will have had time to get over the shock of her cousin's death and Poullet will be numbed to the sound of her wailing and crying. Who knows, he might even be less belligerent," Paul suggests.

"Fat chance," I reply. "But I hope you're right because we'll have to interview them separately, and you're having Poullet."

His shocked expression freezes his face and his hand covers his mouth.

"Please, Boss, no! He scares the life out of me and he hates me. I'll do anything. I'll wash your car. I'll take you out to lunch after the interviews, and I'll pay. I'll do your filing. Please, please, anything but Poullet." Paul kneels on the floor, hands clasped as if in prayer. "Anything," he begs.

"He doesn't hate you Paul," I say laughing. "He hates everyone! You can beg all you like, but you're still getting Poullet. I've socialised with him, so I'm too close. We must be seen to be impartial. However, thanks for your kind offers, but my car is clean; we won't have time for lunch and you do most of my filing anyway."

He stands, sighs and hangs his head in resignation.

"Right, Paul, let's get out of here while there's still some of Saturday left," I say solemnly. "When you get home, rest up. You'll need all your strength for Monday."

His reply does not require words. Just a single-fingered gesture.

When I arrive home Ollee is lying beside the front door in the shade. His head is resting on his paws and, as I approach, he opens his eyes, lifts his ears and wags his tail. He is obviously comfortable as he doesn't rise, but instead rolls onto his back, legs in the air, belly exposed. He turns his head towards me and sighs as if this small movement is all he can manage. As I stop beside him, he stares into my eyes and gives a small 'yip', begging for a tummy rub.

"Oh my, what a lazy lump you are," I say, and oblige him by ruffling his chest fur and tickling his belly.

He shuts his eyes, and one of his back legs shakes with pleasure.

"What an easy life you have," I say. If only everything in life was this simple, I think.

As I enter the house, rich cooking smells assault my nostrils. I detect a delicious mixture of aromas; as well as meat and fried onions, there is the sugary, buttery scent of one of Patricia's fruit pies.

"Honey, I'm home," I call, copying the phrase from a movie.

"Dinner will be on the table in five minutes," Patricia shouts from the kitchen. "I've set the table in the garden and the wine is breathing."

I inhale deeply and then slowly blow the air out again, instantly feeling relaxed. I too can breathe, now that I'm in the sanctuary of our home.

Reaching up, I light the oil lamp which is suspended over the centre of the table from the pergola. It is barely evening, but darkness descends early in Autumn. Bunches of grapes still hang from the vines above our heads and the yellowing leaves throw shadows over everything beneath. While we eat, inevitably, our conversation is about the hanged man.

"Why would someone kill him in that way?" Patricia asks. "It's so odd. Why not just shoot him and be done with it? Much simpler than making him drive up the mountain in his car with a ladder. The killer must have had a gun or another weapon to force Poullet's cousin to comply. Why else would he hang himself?"

"You've answered your own question," Patricia. "The killer wanted him to hang himself, to take his own life. He wanted Henri to know that he'd done something terribly wrong and to feel remorse. I'm sure this killing was personal. Betrayal perhaps. We're looking for someone with a grudge. At least we will be, once the powers that be rule out it being a simple suicide."

"Marjorie came by to visit earlier," Patricia says, changing the subject. "I was only home for five minutes before she arrived."

"How is she? What did our illustrious mayor's wife want? Did she come to buy some produce from you? She usually telephones to see if we're going to be in before dropping in."

Hanging Around in the Pyrenees

"Actually, she was very upset. She was no sooner through the door than she burst into tears."

"What's happened? Is she ill? Is there a problem with one of the children?"

"The problem is with her rotten husband. As you know, he's been having an affair with a younger woman for some time. Marjorie is my best friend, after you of course, and I can't understand why she puts up with it."

"Look, Patricia, everyone knows he's having an affair," I reply, "but at least he keeps his mistress away from his family and their friends. He doesn't flaunt her in public. Marjorie puts up with it because she enjoys the position of being the mayor's wife. She lives a privileged life, both socially and financially. Being married to a cheating bastard like Francis has its compensations, so what's causing her grief? What's changed?"

"He just gave his mistress a job in his office. She is his new PA," Patricia says. Her face is stiff with indignation and she stares into my eyes.

"Oh merde," I reply. "No wonder she's upset."

"Marjorie feels she cannot enter the Mairie now. Everyone who works there will know. She's frightened the town staff will be mocking her behind her back. She's scared that this is just the first step and perhaps Francis will try to replace her in their home too."

I can't quite believe Francis has done this. He had the perfect set up. Why risk everything? His brains are certainly not in his head, I think.

Marjorie has been our close friend for some time now, but her husband has always been distant. Even though Marjorie's brother is gay, Francis is homophobic and has always kept Patricia at arm's length. I'm sure he still sees us as a couple while everyone else accepts us as we really are, as sisters not lovers. I have done favours for him and helped him, so he owes me. When I go to bed, I can't stop thinking about the situation. Perhaps I should talk to him and try to make him see sense. Something must be done before everything spins out of control. I rely on my close relationship with the mayor to keep the status quo in this town, and to support my extra-curricular work. I mustn't let the fool do anything that will put pressure on my position.

* * *

I have a very sleepless night, then I wake early on Sunday morning. It's still dark outside. Patricia is going to Montpellier with her friend Elodi, who is a savonniere. An elderly woman who also makes soap is retiring. She has offered to sell Elodi her remaining stock and some equipment at a knock down price. However, the lady is leaving for Paris early in the afternoon and it will take some time to load Elodi's van. The journey should take about two hours each way. So, it's a very early start for my friend. I don't hear her rise, or move about in the kitchen preparing her breakfast. Neither do I hear Elodi's van draw up or the front gate open. But Ollee does, and the little dog barks his head off. I'm sure he will wake the neighbours for miles around. Ollee barking for France at six o'clock on a Sunday morning is not going to make us popular.

"Sorry, I'm so sorry, Danielle," Patricia calls. She knows I'll have been woken. "Quiet, Ollee, please stop; go back to your bed. Bed, now," she insists.

Then I hear the front door close and silence resumes. I think about trying to go back to sleep, but it is no use. I'm awake now, so I decide to plan my working week as there is much to do both in the office and in our home before we wind down for winter. By ten, I've walked the dog, picked up a fresh baguette for breakfast and although I'm tired, I feel better for having sorted out my agenda. I decide to phone Poullet to arrange the earliest time to hold the interviews with him and his wife.

The call is answered on the third ring, so I know he's been awake.

"Yes. Who is it?" he says.

"Bonjour Doctor, ca va?" I ask. "It's me, Danielle."

"Danielle," he repeats. "Are you ill?" he asks. "Have you fallen in the street and can't get up? Are you having a heart attack?"

His voice is gruff and grumpy.

"I'm fine – thank you," I reply hesitantly.

"Do you know what time it is? What day it is? It's Sunday," he bellows. "The Lord's day. A day for church and rest. Why are you calling me?"

"You don't go to church and you rest most days," I say cheekily. "I might be calling to invite you to lunch. I might be phoning to have a chat with you about something you're interested in."

"And is that the case?" he asks, chuckling now.

"No, I'm phoning to make an appointment to interview you and your wife about Henri Boudin."

"Tomorrow morning – ten thirty – not one minute before."

The line goes dead. He has hung up without saying au revoir. Silly old fool I think. No wonder Paul's scared of him.

Chapter 4

When I arrive at the office on Monday, Paul has opened up and is sitting at his desk surrounded by papers. Marie-Therese, my latest recruit, is making coffee.

"Morning, Boss," Paul says. "As you can see, I'm drowning under paperwork this morning." He sweeps his arm over the desk with a flourish. "So, Marie-Therese has volunteered to go with you to interview the Poullets. It will be good experience for her." He smiles at the newest recruit and winks and she nods her head enthusiastically.

"I don't know what this sneaky devil has told you or promised you," I say, addressing her, "but Paul is coming with me this morning. Didn't anyone ever tell you never to volunteer?" She stares at the floor and is obviously embarrassed. Paul has a way with the ladies, but his charm doesn't work on me. I make my way towards my inner office. "Shame on you," I say as I pass his desk, and at least he has the good grace to blush.

Later, as we head for Poullet's house, we walk past the creperie. A young couple are sitting outside eating gallettes piled with scrambled eggs and cheese. The aroma of their sweet, dark coffees reaches my nostrils and I remember that it has been several hours since I've eaten. Paul licks his lips and he looks longingly at the food. A month before there would not have been an empty table here and people would have been queueing to get a seat. The town would have been full of annoying tourists with their loud voices, drunken behaviour and horribly bad-mannered children. That's the price we must pay in order to bring money into our town. Four months of hell in exchange for eight months of relative peace.

I hear Paul's stomach rumble.

"Have you not eaten yet?" I ask.

"No, Boss, too nervous; it wouldn't do if I threw up over Poullet."

I notice that his eye has developed a tic. I have seen Paul deal with murderers and madmen. I can't understand why one fat, old doctor scares him so much, but he obviously does.

"About that, Paul," I say. "I've decided that we'll both interview each of them. I'll ask the questions and you take the notes." I can't bear his discomfort any longer.

Paul says nothing, but looks as if he might weep with relief. Then he throws his arms around me, before cupping my face in his hands and kissing me on both cheeks.

"Paul," I cry, wriggling out of his grasp. "For heaven's sake. We're in uniform. That kind of behaviour is not appropriate."

But the truth is, I'm delighted we have such a good relationship. When you work in a small office, situated in a small spa town, good working relationships are very important.

We arrive at Poullet's door at precisely ten thirty-five. He opens it immediately. I'm sure he's been hovering behind it, waiting. He makes a show of looking at his watch.

"You're late," he grumbles.

We are forced to squeeze past his enormous bulk to enter the house.

"Front room," he barks.

"Where is your wife?" I ask.

"Why, in the kitchen, of course," he replies, staring at me as if I'm an idiot.

"We would like to speak to her now, please," I say in as formal a tone as I can muster. "We wish to interview her first."

He huffs, turns, then disappears out of the door. We follow him and proceed down a narrow, dark hallway, unsure if this is what is expected of us.

"The police are here, my dear," he announces, as he enters the kitchen. It's the first time he has spoken gently.

Madame Poullet is a plump, soft-looking woman. She epitomises everything I would expect of a grandmother from the rolls of grey curls that frame her rosy-cheeked face, to her lavender-scented perfume. The kitchen is clearly her domain. Morning sun shines through the rear window. A large dining table in the centre of the room is set with fresh, buttery croissants and a jug of coffee.

"Do sit down," she invites. "My husband told me earlier that you wish to speak to us separately. He'll wait in the front room until you're ready for him."

Her eyes flash with steely determination and Poullet positively shrinks under her glare. I'm surprised, and Paul can't supress a smirk. Well, well, I think, maybe this is the reason why he bullies everyone else. Maybe she is the boss in their home.

"Do help yourself. I made this for you," she says, indicating to the food on the table.

The words are barely out of her mouth before Paul is munching happily on a croissant.

We go through the formalities; full name, address, date of birth, etc. I establish that Madame Poullet is Henri's next of kin.

"He never married, you see," she explains. "He lived with his elderly parents until they died. Then he sold the family home, moved to Argeles, and retired from work."

"What did he work at before retiring?" I ask.

"He worked tirelessly for a charity. He did so much for the community. He was such a good man. A saint some would say. God rest his soul."

She crosses herself then takes a handkerchief from her pocket and wipes a tear from her eye.

"Please tell me that he didn't kill himself," she pleads, staring from me to Paul. "He was religious, God-fearing; he would never commit such a sin."

"I can't be one hundred percent certain until I hear from Doctor Picard, Madame, but I'm pretty sure Henri was murdered," I reply.

"Oh, mon Dieu," she says, crosses herself again, then bursts into floods of tears.

Paul purses his lips, rolls his eyes at me then reaches for another croissant. It's clear this won't be a short visit. When she finally manages to compose herself, I continue.

"What was the exact nature of his charity work?" I probe.

"He, together with a couple of his friends, ran a sort of halfway home for delinquent boys. Teenagers who were in trouble. They would normally be put into some type of institution, or prison establishment, but Henri offered the home as an alternative. His work was highly praised, and he had much success in rehabilitating the young men. The home only closed about three years ago and Henri retired."

"Why did the home close," I ask. "Were there any problems?"

Her mouth is down turned, and she throws me a hard stare. "Of course, there were no problems," she snaps. "I've already told you, my cousin was a saint. It was simply down to money. The home relied on its patrons and donations for the day to day running costs. These are hard times and the money dried up, so they were forced to close. There were never any problems," she stresses.

Paul glances at me and raises his eyebrows. It is obvious to me that he too thinks we're not being told the whole story.

We thank Madame Poullet for her help and allow her to lead us back to the front room where the doctor is pacing the floor.

"I hope this won't take much time," he says when we are seated. "Things to do, places to be," he grumbles. "I take it you've both heard about Saint Henri and his stalwart toil for the community? I don't know what I can add."

"It seems to me that you didn't have much time for the man," I say.

"He was odd," Poullet replies, his mouth is pursed with distaste. "He made my skin crawl. Too kind and smarmy to be true. I didn't trust him. There were rumours about him. He didn't marry and, from what I've heard, he didn't have a girlfriend – ever. But then you know how people like to gossip."

"So, you don't know of any reason why someone would want to kill him?" I ask.

"No specific reason – no. But you might want to interview his ex-colleagues; perhaps they can throw fresh light on your investigation. As well as Henri, there were two others who were heavily involved. Then there were the board of governors. Our mayor was on the board for at least four years, as were several local business owners. The home was highly regarded, especially in the earlier years. Being associated with it was good for business and for votes."

Our conversation comes to a natural end as I can't think of anything else to ask.

"It's time for you to leave me in peace, now, Danielle," Poullet states, and he stands and makes for the door. There is no room for argument. "You too," he says glaring at Paul. "Unless you're planning on becoming my lodger, in which case you can pay me rent." He holds out his hand as if waiting for money.

Paul jumps to his feet. His eye is twitching again as he bolts out of the door. Poullet is clearly amused, his eyes twinkle and he grins at me.

What a bad old devil he is, I think, but I can't help liking him.

Chapter 5

When I get back to the office I set Paul the task of locating Henri Boudin's contacts. His colleagues' names were the only useful information that the Poullets could give us. It seems that I may have to spread my investigation further afield than this town and the seaside resort of Argeles, where he lived, if I'm to discover who hated him enough to kill him. The police at Argeles have not yet come back to me with details of anyone who he had regular contact with, other than his priest.

One of his previous work colleagues, Valentin Foret, lives quite nearby, and the other man, Roland Michel, resides in a small farmhouse in the mountains behind Maurellias, with his disabled brother and his herd of goats.

I've never liked goats. They have mean eyes and I'm constantly on my guard with them. They always come too close to me and they look as if they might bite. I'll take Marie-Therese with me when I go to that interview, I think. She's a large, robust girl who grew up on a farm, so she's probably used to animals. At the very least, I can use her as a barrier between me and the goats. Paul would be utterly useless; he'd be more frightened than me.

My thoughts go back to what Patricia told me about Marjorie and Francis and I decide to call Francis at the Mairie to arrange a meeting with him. I shut my door, so I'm not disturbed, then filled with trepidation, I dial the number and the phone begins to ring. I'm not sure what I'm going to say. My hands are sweating with nerves and I tightly grip the phone so that it doesn't slip from my hand. On the eighth ring, when I'm about to hang up, I hear a recorded message informing me that Monsieur le Mayor, will be out of the office until Thursday. I am flooded with relief. I shouldn't have tried to call before planning precisely what to say. But now, at least I can make Patricia happy by informing her that I've tried to contact Francis without being forced to speak to him.

At four o'clock, I give my colleagues plenty of work to be getting on with, advise them I'll be available on my mobile, then head for the door. The beauty about being the boss is that I can pretty much make my own hours.

"Going for a siesta, Boss? Are you tired? Think you've done enough work today? Well don't you worry, your slaves will pick up the slack," Paul says. He grins at Marie-Therese. I know he has no interest in the girl, but he can't help showing off to her.

I don't rise to the bait, but smile sweetly at him as I pass his desk before leaving the confines of the office, letting the door slam shut behind me. While making my way to my car, I stop briefly at the wine shop to buy a couple of bottles of locally produced red wine. It's cheap, but has a rich flavour and it is delicious. Patricia and I will enjoy a bottle with our meal later. We might even open it when I get home. I feel that I'm entitled to this free time as Saturday, which should have been my day off, was ruined.

The familiar journey passes in a blur. I could drive this road with my eyes shut. The nearer to home I get, the more relaxed I feel. The leaves on the trees are turning from a thousand different greens to yellows and reds; the vines have been stripped of all but a few of their grapes, and apples have been harvested and stored. The autumn sun still has warmth and it throws a mellow hue over the landscape. I am happy and feel that all is well with the world; that is until I turn a corner and my home comes into view. Abandoned like children's toys, parked at crazy angles, I count four cars and a van in front of my house. Racing me for the last feasible on-street parking space, another woman hastily stops her vehicle, nods in my direction, then jumps out of her car, clutching what looks like three shoe boxes wrapped in pretty paper. She rushes up the driveway and enters my home without stopping to knock on the door first.

I have no idea what's going on. All I know is I'm no longer happy or relaxed. Pulling the car into the driveway, I practically throw myself through the front door. There is a cacophony of noise coming from the kitchen, women laughing and chatting, music playing, wine glasses clinking and Ollee is barking his head off. When they see me, apart from the dog, everyone becomes still and silent.

"Oh, Danielle, it's you," Patricia says. "I didn't expect you home for ages."

"Apparently," I reply, tetchily.

"Come into the sitting room with me and I'll explain," Patricia says. I follow her, inhaling deeply to calm myself and to supress my annoyance at this home invasion. The chatter begins again.

Patricia says, "Do you remember I told you about my friend Jennifer, the English girl who works at the spa?"

I have a vague recollection.

"Well, she's involved with a charity which helps underprivileged and orphaned children in Romania. Her husband is a driver for the charity. He's volunteered to take shoe boxes filled with gifts as Christmas presents for the children. I'm helping Jennifer to co-ordinate the collection of the boxes because we have room in our shed to store them. Today is one of the drop-off days. It feels great to be helping, especially as we don't have any children of our own to spoil."

Patricia's eyes are sparkling. Her heart is full of love for these urchins who she'll never meet or get to know. It's at this moment I realise just how much she would like to have a child in her life. I can give my friend just about anything she desires. We have a great life here in our little house; we are comfortably off and are very happy together, but I can't give her a child, and she is a woman with so much love to give. I've never really thought about us having children in our lives, but I'm thinking about it now.

"I'm sorry I've intruded, darling," I say. "You just continue helping your friend and I'll take Ollee to the orchard to chase rabbits. We'll return in a couple of hours to see how you're getting on."

"Bless you, Danielle. Thank you for being so understanding. I'm sorry I've spoilt the surprise of you coming home early. I'll get rid of this lot as soon as possible then we can relax. You might meet your papa at the orchard. He told me he was going to check on his beehives."

"That is good news," I reply. "I haven't seen him for a couple of weeks. It will be great to catch up, then I can drive him home. It gets dark so early now and it will save him walking."

"I'll see you later then," she says, kissing me on the cheek before returning to the rabble in the kitchen.

When I arrive at our orchard, I'm pleased to see my father is still there. He had worked for us for a couple of years when he was made redundant from his job. It suited us all – he needed the money – we needed his expertise. Now Papa and Patricia work side by side to produce our fruit and nut crops and he also has his beehives. The bees pollenate the trees and the blossoms feed the bees – everybody wins.

"Danielle, bonjour ma petite," he calls as Ollee and I get out of the car. "What brings you here at this time? Aren't you working today?"

"I just finished early today Papa, and Patricia said you might still be here."

"I've been preparing the hives for the winter," he says. "Most of the work was finished last month. Each colony has a young queen, and they've been given sufficient stores to last them until the spring flowers emerge, but I'm making wind breaks to protect the bees from the icy blasts we sometimes get here."

"I didn't know so much was involved. I'm very impressed, Papa. You've become rather an expert."

"Yes, that's true; you must never underestimate your old Papa. I know much more about this and that than you'd ever imagine."

He has a twinkle in his eyes and a broad grin on his face. "Isn't that right Ollee? Isn't that right?" he says rubbing the dog's back vigorously. Ollee responds by taking off at speed and running round and round in ever decreasing circles while barking like mad. We both laugh at his antics.

"I've about another thirty minutes of work to finish off," Papa says. "Fifteen minutes if you can spare the time to assist me. The light is fading fast, so I'd appreciate your help."

"Of course, Papa. Then I'll drive you home. By the way, where is your dog today. You usually bring her with you."

"Your mama has both dogs with her. She is meeting with the new curate and she's been told he's crazy about dogs."

"Even Mama's dog! Everybody hates him. He's ugly, snappy and really bad-tempered, no-one likes Pepe, except Mama, of course."

"I suppose they understand each other," Papa replies, laughing. "She too can be very snappy."

Within a short while we are pulling up outside my parent's home.

"Please come in, Danielle, and say bonjour to your Mama. It will just take a minute and it'll please her."

I feel myself stiffen. I've never really got on with Mama, but at least we can talk to each other now.

"Just for a few minutes then," I agree. "I must get home. Patricia will wonder where I've got to," I lie.

"Danielle, how lovely," Mama says when we enter the house. Her lips smile but her eyes do not.

The house is claustrophobic. We sit in the kitchen, and she offers me coffee which I decline. It's hot and steamy in the room. Something which smells like cabbage is simmering on the stove.

"I've heard that Henri Boudin has been found dead," she says. I know his friend, Roland Michel. He lives in Maurellias with his brother Georges, but they attend church here. Strangely enough, they weren't at church yesterday or the Sunday before. I do hope they aren't ill. Georges relies on Roland. He can't get anywhere without him. He can walk a little with two sticks, but usually he needs a wheelchair – cerebral palsy," she states. "His speech is affected too. He sounds drunk when he speaks. When I was a girl, he probably wouldn't have survived, but everything is different now. We save everyone nowadays."

If you had your way, poor Georges would have been smothered at birth, I think.

"Thanks for the offer of coffee," I say, standing. "But I must get home now. I'm much later than I said I'd be."

"Give our regards to Patricia," she replies. I notice she says regards, not love.

They walk me to the door. Papa cups my face in his meaty hands and kisses me heartily on both cheeks. Mama manages a quick peck on my temple. I'm so relieved to be out of their house that as I drive towards home I sing along with the radio. Ollee howls his appreciation or his disgust. I'm not sure which, but I really don't care.

Chapter 6

By the middle of the week we have all the facts we require to formally confirm that Henri's death was indeed murder. Why couldn't it have been a simple suicide, I think? We were just beginning to wind down after the summer season, now I'll have a huge amount of work to do and I'm cheesed off. I advise my superior in Perpignan, but as expected, he leaves me and my team to investigate. No help from him then. Paul has telephoned the number he has for Valentin Foret, but is greeted with a recorded message informing him that Monsieur Foret is on retreat in Spain and cannot be reached until his return next week. The number for Roland Michel goes straight to an answerphone.

"What do people do on retreat?" Paul asks. "Is it just an excuse to get together with your pals for a drunken party?"

"It's more likely to seek calmness and quiet for religious reflection," Marie-Therese replies, piously.

"Oh, get you!" Paul says. "Who died and made you Mother Superior?"

She stares at him with a serious expression. "My sister is a nun. She's in a closed order and I only get to see her once a year. I miss her," she adds, holding her hand over her mouth and looking as if she might cry.

"Oh, mon Dieu, I'm so sorry. I didn't mean to offend you. Please don't be upset. I'm an idiot," Paul splutters. His face is bright red.

There is an awkward silence for a moment before Marie-Therese guffaws with laughter.

"Yes, you are an idiot," she replies "and gullible too. You should think before you open your mouth."

"So, your sister isn't a nun?"

"No, you fool, she's an actress. She's on the telly. Her stage name is Claire Amour. She'll be playing the stripper in the new soap which starts next month."

"About as far away from a nun as you can get then," Paul says stiffly, and we explode with laughter.

My, my, I think, well done Marie-Therese; the kitten has claws after all. Paul better watch his step.

As we can't interview Valentin Foret until next week we decide to visit Roland Michel. I leave Paul to make the arrangements as I've decided he'll be accompanying me, in spite of us both being scared of the goats we might encounter there. But after thirty minutes he enters my room.

"Roland's phone probably needs charged," he says. "I've tried calling several times but I'm just getting a recorded message after the first ring. I did leave a message saying we'll be with him after lunch. With luck, he'll be there, but even if he isn't home, his brother might be in. Then Georges will be able to tell Roland we want to speak to him, or better still, tell us where to find him. From what I've heard, Georges doesn't venture out very often. It seems he's a rather well-known author. He's writing a book on the history of the area, and prefers to stay close to home and his computer."

"We'll drive up in my car, Paul," I say. "I don't fancy our chances on that road in one of the police vans. I looked up an area map on my computer, and according to it, the final section of the route is approximately half a kilometre long and little more than a track. At least my car can handle it as it's a four-wheel drive."

"I love your car, Boss. It'll be like being in a rally on that track. Can I drive?"

"Not a snowball's chance in hell," I reply.

"But you let me drive last week," he protests.

"I'm older and wiser now," I say. "You're driving left me feeling much, much older."

He leaves my room with his shoulders hunched. Chastised by two different women in the space of an hour, poor Paul, I think.

I do hope Roland can give us some sort of lead to follow, because at this precise moment, we have nothing. I've been handed a very small list of past Board members, comprising of one businessmen, a teacher, a priest and Francis. At least now I have an excuse to talk to Francis, so I might get an opportunity to discuss his unacceptable and politically dangerous dalliances.

I'm not sure who, if anyone else, was involved with the home, apart from the former gardener who's now dead, and the former housekeeper who's in an old age home, and, according to the care staff there, is completely gaga with dementia.

I arrange to see Paul at my car at three o'clock. I don't want it to be any earlier as I'd like to try to meet Patricia for lunch. She's been so busy recently overseeing the care of the orchard and the harvest as well as running her pies and pickles business. Now she's trying to produce enough of her paintings for the Christmas sale. Add to that her charity work and spending time supporting Marjorie, not to mention running our household, caring for our chickens, rabbits and our kitchen garden. She's amazing – a superwoman. I respect her so much and love her dearly. I pick up the phone and dial her number.

"Have you got time for lunch?" I ask, when she answers her mobile.

"Oh, I'm so sorry, Danielle," she replies. "I've got Marjorie dropping in for a chat and a sandwich. She'll talk while I keep painting. I've almost finished the commissioned work for the baker's wife, but I've still got lots to do for the Christmas sale. Why don't you come home and join us? It'll just be baguette and brie, but you'll get to see Marjorie as well."

What a good idea, I think. I'll be able to hear about Francis before I speak to him. Perhaps Marjorie can shed some light on his behaviour and why he's suddenly changed. He used to be so discreet and would never have risked hurting his family.

"I'll be home at twelve-thirty. Is that okay?" I ask.

"Perfect. If you walk past the baker, could you pick up some Florentines, please? We'll probably need something sweet and chocolatey."

"No problem, darling. Till later then."

She says, 'bye Cherie', then she's gone.

As I'm about to leave the office, Cedric, one of my officers arrives, saving me a phone call. I explain that I will probably be away for the rest of the afternoon and that Paul will be with me from after the lunch break.

"You'll be the most senior officer here, so you'll have to keep an eye on Marie-Therese," I inform him. "She's meant to have two hours of training today, so she can write it up for her assessment. The work has to be more than just filing."

"What did you have in mind, Boss?" he asks, staring deep into my eyes and smiling. He rather unnerves me as he's startlingly good looking, tall and broad with serious, green eyes and bright auburn hair. He looks more like a model than a policeman.

"That's the problem, Cedric," I answer, quickly composing myself. I can't think of anything to give her. It's a quiet time of year and apart from the murder investigation, which is at a very early stage, the most taxing things we have on the books are a missing dog and a dispute over a private walkway. With regards to the home where Henri Boudin worked, Paul and I are contacting the people connected to it, so that only leaves the teenagers who were placed there. I'm hoping we'll have our answers before we must speak to any of them."

"Why don't I set Marie-Therese the task of finding the old records. Then if we do need to get in touch with former residents, we'll have the information at our fingertips," he suggests.

"I'm not sure if any records still exist," I reply. "The home's been closed for some time now."

"Then it will be good investigative police work for her to search for them; it'll take her hours, days maybe. And, as we're so quiet, I'll read the newspaper and sit with my feet up drinking coffee while she gets on with it. You won't have to concern yourself about her training because I'll be here to oversee. Everybody wins!"

He is chuckling to himself and I too find myself laughing at his cheek. Cedric is normally rather quiet. He just gets on with the job, but from time to time he's funny and he's as sharp as a knife when it comes to police work.

"I'll leave her in your safe hands then," I say, and I exit the office with a smile on my face and a spring in my step.

* * *

When I arrive home, Marjorie's car is already there. I can see Ollee lying in the shade under his favourite shrub, gripping a large bone between his paws and working determinedly with his tongue to extract the marrow from it. Mimi, our cat, is stretched close by in the sunshine. At least Ollee has the good grace to welcome me. He gives a single 'yip', runs over and briefly licks my hand, sniffs the bag of cakes, then returns to his bone. Mimi ignores me as usual. She doesn't even stir. I am only of interest to her when I'm opening her food.

As I enter the house both Patricia and Marjorie greet me with a kiss.

"Come and sit at the table, Danielle," Patricia says. "There's baguette, brie, fig chutney, charcuterie and fruit. And now we have chocolate," she adds, taking the bag of Florentines from me and placing them on a plate.

"How are things with you, Marjorie?" I ask.

I have uttered the words before noticing the warning look from Patricia. Marjorie pushes back her chair, stands and walks over to the window, her back to us. She takes a handkerchief from her pocket and dabs at her eyes.

"She's very fragile," Patricia hisses. "Please watch what you say to her."

After a couple of moments, she returns and sits down.

"I'm so sorry," she says. "Please excuse my behaviour."

"Don't apologise," I reply. "We're your friends. Why don't you tell us what this is all about? We might be able to help you," I offer.

She inhales deeply, blows her nose, then begins.

"I no longer love Francis," she states. "He's the father of my children, but that's all. He has hurt me so much over the years that I've grown to dislike him intensely. Now he's flaunting his newest mistress in my face and I cannot bear it. I want to leave him, but I can't. Everything I have is tied to him. The house we live in was bought with the inheritance I received from my father. I stupidly bought it in our joint names, even though all the money was mine. I was in love then." She explains, and gives a wry smile. "All his wages go into his account; then he transfers money into mine to cover the bills and my expenses. The only income that is exclusively mine comes from my trust fund, but that wouldn't be enough to live on. So, you see, I'm stuck with him."

She dabs at her eyes then begins again.

"Now he's talking about renting out our basement, studio flat. We've only ever kept it for guests. We don't need the income. I think he's planning to move his mistress in there. He's already got her working for him at the Mairie."

"Have you met this woman? Do you know what she's like?" I ask.

"Oh, yes, I've met her. I was in town sitting at the Café de Paris, waiting for the rest of the people on the charity committee to arrive for a meeting, when she approached me. 'Marjorie,' she said, 'how nice to finally meet you, I've heard so much about you from Francis. I do hope we can be friends. I'm Monique.' Then she grinned at me and held out her hand for me to shake. Can you imagine how I felt? She called me by my first name. She thought I'd want to be her friend. The woman who's stealing my husband. Any of the committee could have arrived at any moment and my husband's mistress was speaking to me as if everything was normal."

"What a bitch!" Patricia exclaimed. "What a brazen hussy!"

"What did you do?" I ask.

"For a moment I was shocked, then I just wanted be rid of her before anyone else arrived. So, I stood up and gripped her outstretched hand – tightly – very tightly. I could see by the look on her face that I was hurting her. Then I crushed her hand some more. She tried to pull away, but I didn't let her. I only just stopped short of breaking her bones. Then I pulled her towards me and spoke softly in her ear. 'Don't you ever approach me again,' I said. 'If you come near me or my home, I'll have you killed. And don't think that Francis will be able to help you because he won't. I have dangerous, powerful, friends who he knows nothing about. If you tell him about this conversation, I'll have them hurt you. – Got it?' She shrank before my eyes. 'Well?' I asked. 'Yes, yes, I've got it,' she replied. Then I twisted her wrist for good measure before releasing her hand, and she scuttled off."

"And do you have dangerous, powerful friends?" I ask.

"No, of course not; you are the toughest friend I have," she replied. "But Monique doesn't know that."

She begins to laugh and cry at the same time and we can't help smiling too.

"I didn't know you could be so tough," Patricia says.

"Neither did I," Marjorie replies. "It's survival instinct, I guess."

Patricia pours coffees and we eat some lunch before I probe a bit further.

"What has brought about this change in Francis? You always knew he played away from home occasionally. It didn't seem to bother you in the past because he always loved you and he would never risk his family. What's different now?"

"He had a heart attack last year," Marjorie replies. "Nobody knew about it. We kept it a secret, so people wouldn't treat him differently, but that's when he changed. This new mistress is in her twenties. I'm sure he finds it all very flattering. What sixty-year-old man wouldn't want sex with a much younger woman?"

Now I think, I'm beginning to understand. This situation is dangerous. If Monique has influence over Francis to this extent – where will it all end? Perhaps he will move her into the studio flat, but worse still, perhaps she'll assist him when he makes important decisions at the Mairie. Then where would that leave me? In my job, I need the backing of the mayor. I hope I won't be forced to choose between my friend Marjorie or her useless husband?

Chapter 7

I find it difficult to drag myself away from Marjorie and Patricia. I'd much rather stay home all afternoon instead of driving up some mountain track in the middle of nowhere. When I do leave, I arrive at the car park to meet Paul nearly ten minutes late. He is leaning against the perimeter wall, with his legs crossed at the ankles, munching an ice cream cornet.

I call to him through the open window. "That looks good," I say.

"It is," he replies.

"What flavour is it?" I ask.

"'Gingembre'."

"That's my favourite," I say.

"Yes, I know," he replies. "That's why I bought it."

"Did you not buy one for me?"

"Yes, I did," he says popping the last morsel into his mouth. "That was it. I've just finished it and it was delicious. I had chocolate ice cream."

He laughs at the dismayed look on my face, then looks pointedly at his watch.

"You're ten minutes late. Ice cream waits for no man – or woman."

"You're turning into Doctor Poullet," I reply. "And you'll become as fat as he is, if you continue to eat for two."

"Oh, dear, Boss, you're not showing the nicest side of your nature. Do you want me to go and buy you another ice cream?"

"No thank you," I reply, sniffily; then I stare at him and make pig-like grunts as he climbs into my car.

"Definitely not the nicest side of your nature," he laughs.

As we begin to drive, dark cloud rolls in from over the Canigou mountain, and by the time we reach the edge of town, the sky is blackening, and thunder is rumbling. We don't get rain very often, and even though I've lived here all my life, it still surprises me that the weather can change so quickly from bright sunshine to monsoon-like rain.

"Merde, that's all we need," Paul says. "We're driving to the back of beyond in a thunder storm. Why couldn't the bad weather have waited until tonight, when I'll be indoors watching the rugby on the television, with my two friends, beer and chips?"

The rain becomes so heavy that the streets resemble a river, and by the time we turn onto the track leading to Roland Michel's home, I can barely differentiate between it and the land that surrounds it. Even with the windscreen wipers going at double speed, it becomes very difficult to see more than a couple of metres in front of me.

"I bet you're glad you're not the one driving, now," I say.

"I'll drive if you want me to, Danielle," Paul says kindly. "Or if you prefer, we can turn around and go back to the office. Tomorrow is another day."

"Thanks for your chivalrous offer, Paul, but we've come this far. So, I'll carry on. We must be about halfway along this track by now."

We continue slowly, trying to avoid any large potholes that have appeared as the rain dislodges rocks along the way.

"Stop, Boss," Paul yells, suddenly. And I brake sharply. "There's something on the road ahead," he says. "Can you see it? It's lying on the right-hand side of the track. Is it an animal?"

I edge the car forward.

"Oh, mon Dieu, It's a person, Paul. A man, not an animal."

Paul and I leap from the car and run forward. Then we spot a wheelchair, on its side, a few yards beyond the man.

"It's Georges Michel," Paul says.

When we reach Georges, I can see that he's very distressed. He clutches my arms and sobs with relief. The poor man is soaked through and shivering.

"Thank God, you came," he says. "I've been stuck here for over two hours."

"Let us help you to my car," I suggest. "You can tell us all about it when we get you indoors and out of this rain."

George lets us carry him to the car, and between us, we manage to manoeuvre the sodden man into the back seat. Then Paul retrieves the wheelchair.

"One of the wheels was stuck in a rut," he says to me. "It's buckled." There's no way Georges could have got any further in it as it is., even if he could have righted it."

When we arrive at the house and get Georges inside, Paul helps the shivering man to his bedroom and assists him in getting changed. Georges' wet trousers are stuck to his legs, and with his condition, it's difficult for him to remove them himself. I fill the coffee maker and switch it on then search for milk. That's when I notice there's not a shred of food in the house and there is no fuel for the log burning stove.

When we are seated at the table drinking hot, black coffee, Georges explains the predicament in which he found himself.

"Roland was going to St Laurent for six days. A man who lives there had work for him, supervising the clearing of some trees on the mountain behind his home, to make a fire break. He had a team of four young men to do the work, but he was going to be away, so he needed an overseer."

He pauses to sip some coffee. Tears flow down his cheeks again.

"Roland's been gone for ten days. He's not been in touch the entire time he's been away. I tried to call him three days ago, but I dropped the phone and it slid below the stove," he says, indicating where it went. "I'm not completely helpless, but there's no way I could retrieve it from under there. So, you see, I had to try to make it down the mountain to my neighbour who lives at the bottom of the track, as I've run out of food. I'm very worried about Roland. He'd never leave me stuck like this. Something must be wrong."

A cold chill runs down my spine and the hairs on the back of my neck stand up. Something is indeed wrong, I think, and with Roland's connection to Henri Boudin, I'm dreading what it might be.

We call social services and explain the situation with Georges. They assure me that someone will arrive within an hour and they'll arrange temporary accommodation and a much-needed meal for him. They can also provide a wheelchair until his can be repaired. I let Georges know that he'll be safe now, and I give him the only food I have in the car, a bar of chocolate and a packet of peanuts. He gives me the contact details of the man who hired Roland. He also gives me a rough idea of the location of the land where Roland was meant to be working.

"What do you think the chances are of someone being here in an hour?" Paul asks, when we are back at the car.

"About zero," I reply.

"Poor soul," Paul says. "He's got a brilliant brain trapped in a useless body. How frustrating it must be for him."

"Yes, and now I fear something's happened to his brother," I say. "Try calling the phone number for Monsieur La Croix, the land owner. I bet it no longer exists."

Paul taps in the number, listens for a moment, then holds the phone to my ear. 'We cannot connect you to this number.' A disembodied voice states.

"Thought so," I say, and I feel a jag of disquiet and impending doom.

I drive Paul home as the weather is so bad. We arrange to meet in the office in the morning to make plans for the day. We must try to locate Roland Michel. This will mean a trip up the mountain to the location Georges has given us.

"Make sure you wear sturdy boots," I advise him. "I think we may have to walk over some very rough ground."

"You think he's dead. Don't you, boss?" Paul says.

"I'm not sure," I reply. "But he's certainly not showing any sign of life. You heard Georges. Roland would never abandon him if he could possibly help it."

"I'd better bring a menthol-infused face mask as well then," he replies. "I can't stand the smell of death."

I park outside his house and he climbs out of the car.

"I'll make sure I eat a hearty breakfast tomorrow, in case I don't fancy lunch. Death is never very appetising," he laughs.

Somehow, we always manage to keep even the most dire situations light-hearted.

Chapter 8

I have a sleepless night. I seem to only nod off for ten or fifteen minutes at a time before waking again. My mind is too active. What with the murder and the missing man, and my worries over Francis, my stress levels are rising, and I feel that things are beginning to spiral out of control. It's just fortunate that Henri and Roland are not important men, otherwise there would be officials clamouring for answers and I'd be under time pressure as well.

After much tossing and turning, I finally give up and rise at five-thirty. Ollee is very happy to see me downstairs and he runs to the front door full of excitement when I suggest a walk. He is less happy when he realises it's still dark, and he stays close to my side. For some reason, I always expect dogs to have good vision, and in daylight, Ollee has, but his night vision is very poor. As we walk he barks at shadows, parked cars, even a shrub blowing in the breeze. He is nervous and jumpy, and I find myself getting spooked too.

"Time to go home for breakfast, boy," I say, and he spins round excitedly his tail rotating with delight and I'm sure, with relief.

When we return to the house the shutters are open and the light is on downstairs.

"Oh, merde, boy, we've woken Patricia," I say.

Ollee responds with an excited 'yip'. Patricia is his favourite person in the world.

When I open the door, she is there, standing in front of me.

"Danielle, are you okay?" she asks, her face full of concern. "I was worried when I woke up and you were both gone. I thought I heard someone moving about in the house, and when I rose, I realised it must have been you and Ollee.

It's very early. Did you get a call from the emergency services? Did you have to go to work?"

"No, Darling, nothing like that. I'm sorry, but I just couldn't sleep. I'm worried about Marjorie and Francis. I'm not sure how to help them."

I tell her the truth, but not the whole truth; Marjorie and Francis are a small part of the pressure I'm under. But why worry my friend?

"You're very kind, Danielle, but we can't have you getting sleepless nights over them. I'm sure the situation will sort itself out one way or another. From what I've heard, Francis' girlfriend has already had a relationship with another official at the Mairie. She moved on to Francis because he was a bigger fish, and a bigger fool, it seems. She's nothing more than a power-grabbing little whore. I'm sure she'll move on again when someone better comes along."

"You're probably right," I reply.

But her words only add to my concerns, as in small-town France, the mayor is the biggest fish, and I can't let this situation continue for long or control will slip from my grasp.

* * *

When I enter the office, it's busy. Cedric is trying to calm down an irate tourist who's been given a parking ticket which he thinks is unjustified.

"This is a matter for the municipal police not the gendarmes, they've issued the ticket. You must speak to the policeman at the desk next door." Cedric says, but the man is having none of it. He is obstinately continuing to argue. "If you don't leave now," Cedric continues, "I'll be forced to arrest you for causing a disturbance."

Paul is talking to the lady whose dog was missing - better news here – the dog has turned up and is being cared for at a kennels on the edge of town. And Marie-Therese is dealing with a man who's reporting an accident that's blocking a minor road.

Within ten minutes, all the problems have been dealt with and Paul and I are on our way to try to locate the house and land of Monsieur La Croix, and perhaps Roland Michel.

It takes us over an hour driving up the mountain to our destination. The rain has dislodged many small rocks and they pepper the road. The surrounding terrain is full of contrasts. The dark green of the evergreen trees interspersed with vibrant reds and yellows of the deciduous trees create a natural tapestry, and every so often, a jagged, coral and grey coloured rock face dominates the landscape.

"Are you sure this is the right location," I ask Paul when we arrive. The house in front of us is semi-derelict, but the land surrounding it is well tended.

"It's the co-ordinates we've been given. The same as Roland Michel had."

"Something is wrong," I say. "He's been led on a wild goose chase, and so have we. Where the hell can he be?"

I call the office and Marie-Therese answers.

"I'm glad you phoned, Boss. I was just about to contact you. There's been an emergency call. The pompiers have already been dispatched to the scene. And Doctor Poullet too. A hunter contacted the emergency services. He's found a car about a ten-minute drive from where you are, two cars, in fact. One of them has a body inside and the other is at risk of going over the edge of the mountain."

"Why was Doctor Poullet asked to attend when the scene is so far from where he lives? He must be moaning insufferably about that," I reply.

"Yes, Boss, he was very grumpy, but he was the only doctor available. He did say something about being paid for using a taxi service as he wouldn't drive that journey in his own car. I think a gentleman called Monsieur Junot is driving him," she adds.

I feel really annoyed. "Junot is not a gentleman," I snap. "He's a journalist and he's a pain in the ass. Call the pompiers. Tell them that if they arrive before me, not to let Junot anywhere near the scene. I suspect the corpse will be Roland Michel. We could be looking at a double murder here. I don't want him reporting his spin on things until we know what's going on."

When we arrive at the scene, I immediately see a fire truck and when I open my door, I can smell the cloying, putrid odour of death. Paul is already turning green.

"Better get those face masks, Paul," I suggest, and make sure you keep the car windows and doors shut or I'll never get rid of the stench."

The pompiers have attached a chain to the precariously parked car and are hauling it from the edge of the drop. I'm delighted to see that my friend, Jean, is in charge. We met for the first time a few years ago and several times since, often at murder scenes. He jokingly calls me 'the kiss of death'. I also see that Poullet has arrived. He must have been summoned before me to get here so quickly. He is grumbling as usual, and as I approach him and Jean, I hear him complain.

"Why have I been called here, Jean? The car is a bloodbath. The flies buzzing about can be heard from fifty metres away. Hovering vultures are fainting with the smell and falling from the sky. Of course, the man is dead. You could have simply telephoned me, and I would have taken your word for it and declared him dead. There was no need for me to travel up this mountain with that babbling monkey, Junot. He listens to rap music, he smells of body odour and he talks a load of rubbish. I thought we were friends, Jean. You could have spared me this torture."

"Poullet," Jean replies, rubbing his forehead with exasperation. "You know a doctor must examine the body and declare it dead at the scene. You have to be here."

"Well, I'm not going anywhere near it," Poullet grumbles. "I officially declare that the man is dead, and I can do nothing to revive him."

"Hello, gentlemen," I say as I approach, and they both turn to greet me.

"Ah, Danielle," Poullet says, "Long time, no see," he quips.

"I heard you complaining about Junot," I say. "Why didn't you use an official taxi then you would have been spared his company and you could have claimed the journey on expenses." I know how he feels about his expenses and it amuses me to wind him up.

"You know that Junot is my official driver at this point in time. I'm employing him. I will be claiming him on my expenses and you will accept the charge." His face is getting redder.

Jean and I exchange glances and he begins to chuckle.

"Very funny, Danielle," Poullet says, spluttering. "Don't upset me today," he warns.

His eyes are serious, and his expression is strained. I am reminded that he has lost a family member in terrible circumstances and I feel chastised.

"Do we know who the corpse is?" Poullet asks. "I take it you've realised that the second car is Henri's?"

I hadn't realised this and I'm shocked I missed the obvious.

"That idiot, Junot, has been taking pictures on his telephone as well as with his camera. I'm sure he's emailed them somewhere," Poullet advises. "Don't let him report anything that will upset my wife, Danielle. Nothing that will show her sainted cousin in a bad light. Not until we know something for sure, please. Junot's already speculating that we have a serial killer on the loose and we don't want his ramblings to cause panic in the streets, do we?"

Indeed, we do not, I think, and I immediately send Paul to speak to the little rat.

"Can you tell me anything about the corpse, Doctor?" I ask. "Is there any obvious sign of how he died? I know you don't want to get too close, and I don't blame you, there's so much blood and the stink is indescribable."

"All I can tell you is that the blood looks black and congealed, so he's been there for some time. I can see slashes to the wrist on his left side. The way his arms are hanging down, the blood ran into the footwell of the car. I assume the other wrist is slashed too. There's an empty vodka bottle lying in the blood and pill bottles as well. Like Henri, it's been made to look like suicide, but I suspect it is not. You know I cannot deal with this corpse because of the cars being found together. It's more than likely the two deaths will be a connected."

"Yes, Doctor," I reply. "I'm sure they are. I think the corpse is Roland Michel, Henri's previous work colleague."

"Oh, mon Dieu, Junot is right, after all. We do have a serial killer on the loose. I wonder who he'll target next. You'd better warn the others who worked at the home or who were on the board of directors."

This thought had also occurred to me. I know who the potential victims could be, but no idea who'd want to kill them. Perhaps getting Marie-Therese to search for the records wasn't such a bad idea after all. If we can find the names of the boys who resided at the home and a list of the companies who supplied it with services, we might discover someone who has a grudge or a score to settle.

Chapter 9

Paul and I are rather subdued. We exchange little conversation on the journey back to the office. The weight of my responsibility is crushing. When we arrive, I make straight for my office and shut the door. I need time alone to think about what to do next. Being the boss is wonderful when times are quiet. I simply let my staff get on with the day to day running of things and I take home the largest pay packet, but it's a different ball game when something major comes along. At times like this, I'm in the spotlight and must earn my keep. Outwardly, I may seem strong, but inwardly I'm quaking like a scared child.

I make a to-do list. Firstly, we must trace Valentin Foret, check that his phone message was genuine and he's still alive, and if he is, warn him about the danger he might be in. Secondly, we must warn the men who were on the board of directors because they too, may be at risk. Finally, it is vital we find the records of the home. Without them, we have no suspects. I telephone through to the main office and ask Marie-Therese to come to my room and when she arrives, I invite her to sit and I pour us both coffee.

"How is your search coming along?" I ask. "Have you discovered any information or records from the home?"

"It's taken me quite some time, Boss, but I've spoken to the priest who was responsible for the spiritual needs of the boys. He told me that the record keeper was Valentin Foret. Henri Boudin was responsible for the day-to-day running of the place. Roland Michel oversaw any work that the boys did and their education, and Valentin took care of all the paperwork.

Something else of interest. The priest and Henri were close friends. They attended the same school when they were boys as did Roland and Valentin, but only Henri and the priest were in the same year. Also, none of the men were married, which I thought was rather strange. I did try to warn the priest to be vigilant, but he said he was perfectly safe as no-one in their right mind would commit a sin against a priest. I also asked him to tell us if anyone came forward to the confessional, anyone with troubles regarding Henri. He practically bit my head off. He said anything said in confession was secret and if he was asked to absolve a sin, even for something as serious as murder, then it would remain a secret. Mind you, I spoke to him before we knew Roland was dead. He might be more forthcoming if he realised we now have two corpses and he could actually be a target.

Because our mayor was on the board of directors, any important documents were transferred to the Mairie when the home closed. I've spoken to a lady called Sabine who works in the library of the Mairie. She's arranging for me to search through the archives to look for the papers," she pauses and sips her coffee. "Do you think I should go there today?" she asks. "Can you spare me from the office?"

"The research you're doing is vital to our enquiry. It takes precedence over everything else. You've done amazingly well to discover all that you have. I'll be giving you a glowing report on your assessment. I know it must have been tedious work, but it's so important to the case. Well done, Marie-Therese, very well done," I say. "You can spend as long as you like searching the archives, but please be diligent. Find me something to go on."

She stands. She is grinning and glowing with pride. "Don't worry, Boss, if the records we need still exist, I'll find them. I'll get on it right away. I'll work late if necessary."

I look at my watch. The working day is almost over. I love her enthusiasm, but I can't let her be over zealous. I am the only person who gets paid overtime in this office. The budget only stretches so far, and any extra money comes directly to me.

"Go home Marie-Therese," I say. "The work day is over. Start fresh tomorrow."

"But there's still half an hour left," she protests.

"It's been a long day, Marie-Therese. Go back to the main office and tell everyone we're closing early. The next few days will be heavy going and we must be well rested and ready for what lies ahead."

When I enter the main office, everyone is packing up their stuff and shutting down the computers.

"I think you've forgotten that tomorrow's a public holiday, Boss," Paul says. "The Mairie will be shut as will all the other official buildings. Do you want any of us to come into work? Or shall we just be on standby as usual during the holidays?"

Merde, I'd forgotten that this was a long weekend. Even though today is only Wednesday, we'll get nothing done until Monday as everyone will take Friday off as well. This unscheduled extra day is referred to as 'le pont'. The bridge between the actual holiday and the weekend. I should have remembered because Patricia and I are due to visit our friends, Freddy and Anna, tomorrow. They own a vineyard and during their first difficult year, we helped them with their harvest. It was backbreaking work, which thankfully, we've never been called upon to repeat. However, they've never forgotten that we helped them, and we've been invited to celebrate with them every year since. We are due there for lunch to sample 'les vins primeurs'. Celebrating the new wines is an important occasion, and Freddy said he's had a very good year, so it should be a great party.

I turn to face Paul. "You're right," I say, "I'd forgotten. We've been so busy during the last few days, I can hardly remember what day of the week it is. Just a skeleton staff, as arranged, and everyone else on standby. Everyone except me, of course," I add, smiling smugly. "I booked Thursday as a break. So, don't drink tomorrow, Paul," I warn. "You're on standby as my driver in case of any emergency. You might get a call to pick me and Patricia up from our friend's vineyard any time up until six o'clock."

He stares at me open-mouthed.

I explain, "We are planning on staying the night so that both Patricia and I can drink Freddy's excellent wine. But in case something occurs that I must attend to, I'll need a driver, because I can't drive if I'm over the limit."

"I didn't know we could book public holidays as a personal break," he protests.

"That's because you can't," I reply. I can't help grinning at his forlorn face.

"I don't mind being on standby to drive you, Boss," Marie-Therese offers. "I don't drink anyway."

Paul's face lights up.

How kind she is, I think. However, in this instance, if something does kick off, I'll need an experienced officer to support me. It should be safe after six, but not through the day. I rarely get called out in the evening, and if I do, I'll deal with the problem then.

I smile at Marie-Therese and say, "If something serious has to be dealt with, I might need Paul to assist me, as he's a senior officer. In fact, Paul can usually deal with most situations himself," I add. "However, I appreciate your willingness, and if you don't mind, I'd like you to be on standby after six."

I shouldn't really need the girl, but she's delighted to be given the responsibility. I'm pleased to help Marie-Therese. It's still tough for women on the force to be considered equal to the men, and I have high hopes for this young woman. She smart, she's strong and she's a team player. I wish someone had been there to support me in the beginning. Sink or swim, I had no-one to rely on but myself.

* * *

Thursday is a beautiful sunny day. I feel as if I'm packing the car for an expedition instead of for a journey which is only a couple of hours up the road. We have everything we need for our overnight stay, even Ollee's bed, his favourite blanket and some of his toys.

"It's worse than travelling with a child," I protest.

We have gifts for Freddy, Anna and their children. Some of Patricia's pickles, a jar of honey from my papa, a tray containing six fruit pies for the party, the list goes on and on. By the time we're ready to leave, there's barely enough room in the car for us and the dog to squeeze into.

"Are there going to be a lot of people at this party?" I ask.

"Not really," Patricia replies. "It's going to be a child-free zone. Freddy and Anna's kids are staying overnight at a friend's house. Their adult children are babysitting. Anna thought it best as we're all going to be drinking and partying. I think there's going to be about twenty of us. Usually it's the children who make the numbers swell."

"Is everyone expecting to stay the night? Will we be sleeping in the barn with a crowd of drunks?"

"Most people will spend the night, but Freddy told me they've now got plenty of room. He said we won't recognise the place. They've built a large extension to the main house and the barn has been converted as gite-style accommodation. They've made a lot of money from the gite this year and they're fully booked for next year. Lots of tourists want to stay on a French farm."

I'm delighted for them. They're very hard-working and they deserve their success.

As we approach the farm, we can see abandoned cars all along the entrance track. Freddy is there, trying to organise the parking. When I pull up, he walks over to us. He is grinning and holding a large wine glass in his hand.

"Hello, lovely girls," he says. "I've kept you a parking space beside the barn because I knew you'd have stuff to carry. It's the one with the police 'no parking' cone at it," he winks.

I think Freddy has already sampled more than a glass or two of wine; his cheeks are ruddy and he seems rather merry. Before very long, we have parked up, found our allocated room in the main house, unpacked the car and are seated in the garden enjoying an excellent lunch. Anna is a great cook, and as is usual for such occasions, each of the guests has brought something to the table. There are dishes of rabbit stew, meatballs in rich sauce, chicken with fried onions and garlic, roasted 'couer de boeuf' tomatoes, one man, who is a local baker, has brought a dozen fresh, crispy baguettes, and as well as Patricia's fruit pies, there is clafouti, macarons and almond biscuits.

"We won't go hungry, then," one of the guests' quips.

Someone has brought an accordion to the party and before very long we are all singing and dancing. As night falls, Freddy lights a couple of outdoor heaters and we gather round to chat under a star-filled sky. Inevitably, the conversation turns to Henri's murder. Freddy is curious to know what I'm involved in at work as are some of the other guests. When I mention that we've discovered a second body, everyone is all ears.

"My cousin lived at that boys' home for two years," a man named Alain says. "He told me it was hell and the people who ran it were monsters."

Suddenly, all other conversation stops.

"Mon Dieu," Anna says, "What did he do to end up there?"

"He was a bad boy, there's no denying that. He was stealing things, joyriding, and one night he and his friends got drunk, stole a car, and crashed into a shop window. That's when he got sent away. But nevertheless, that place was unfit for purpose. While Eddy was there, one boy died in strange circumstances and another boy committed suicide. They were both fifteen years old, just schoolboys."

"What did he mean when he said that the men running the place were monsters," I ask.

"He said the boys were made to do labouring work and the home got paid for their services. Sometimes they worked twelve-hour shifts. They were meant to be getting an education not being used as slave labour. They were all regularly beaten. Eddy's friend had broken ribs and a punctured lung from one of the beatings. When he was taken to hospital, the doctor was told he fell climbing a tree. Nobody believed him when he informed the staff how he really got injured."

"And do you think he told you the truth? Couldn't he have simply been making up stories?" Anna asks. "You did say he was often in trouble."

"He was telling the truth. There were too many tales about that place for it to be a lie. According to Eddy, the priest who was meant to be looking after their spiritual needs was the worst. He knew what was going on, but didn't intervene. On the contrary, he was a sadistic bully who would supervise much of the torture. Eventually, the home stopped getting donations as more and more stories came to light. The board of directors closed the book on the place and the monsters got off scot free. I'm not surprised two of them are now dead. There were many who'd have wished for it."

"Do you think that one of the former residents might have killed them?" I ask, "And, if so, why wait until now?"

"Who knows," Alain replies. "There are so many potential people to choose from. There are the former residents, their families, local people who thought they were contributing to something good only to find themselves implicated in something awful. Then there are the usual mix of mad men and vigilantes. I don't know what would drive someone to murder. But one thing is certain, there are still potential victims out there. I don't envy your job, Danielle."

On that sombre note, the party comes to a natural end, and apart from a couple of the men who continue drinking with Freddy, everyone heads for their beds.

Chapter 10

On Saturday morning the house is full of chattering women again. It's the last day for people to deliver their shoe boxes for Romania. One lady, whose name is Beatrix, arrives with a small child, a little girl of about five or six years old. The child sidles up to me and quietly slips her hand into mine. She stares at me with saucer-like eyes.

"May I pat your dog?" she asks, shyly.

"Yes, of course," I reply. "Shall I introduce you to him? His name is Ollee."

"Hello, Ollee, lollee," she says, laughing. Then she kneels and rubs his belly.

I leave her to rain affection on my spoilt boy and return to speak to Patricia and Beatrix.

"You're a miracle worker," Beatrix says. "You're the first person she's spoken to since her mother died. I'm her foster carer," she explains. "Ava's been with me for nearly a week and she hasn't uttered a single word. The psychologist thinks she's been very traumatised by the sudden death of her mother. I'm so relieved she's speaking again. I didn't know how to help the poor little soul."

"Has she no family to care for her?" Patricia asks.

"Her aunt is a medical doctor. She normally lives in the family home with her sister and Ava, but she volunteers with Medicines Sans Frontiers whenever she gets a holiday, and it just so happens she's away just now. Ava's mother had an undetected heart condition and she died very unexpectedly."

"How sad," Patricia says. "Will Ava continue to live with her aunt?"

"Oh, yes, she's coming home as soon as she can to be with the child. Probably in a day or two. I'm a temporary foster carer. The longest a child has ever been with me is three months."

"How does your husband feel about that," I ask. "It must be difficult having different children coming and going?"

"Oh, I'm not married," Beatrix says. "I see being a foster carer as a career choice. I love children and I get paid to look after them. I'm also a qualified counsellor, so I can get plenty of private work to boost my income."

I see Patricia looking fixedly at Ava and I wonder what's going on in her mind.

"She's lovely, isn't she?" she says, turning and staring into my eyes.

"Yes, she is," I agree. I hold her stare for a minute before she drops her gaze and turns away.

As more and more people arrive, I decide to take myself out of the house and walk into town. I'm hoping my friend Byron will be at the café reading his newspaper as usual. We've been friends for a few years now, in fact, at one time, apart from Patricia, he was my only real friend. He's English, but I don't hold that against him! He's a stylish, older gentleman with impeccable taste, and he's funny and very supportive. I love Byron, and both Patricia and I treat him as a beloved uncle. He's often the voice of common sense and I like to talk through my ongoing cases with him. I'd value his opinion on what my next move should be to see if we share the same views.

I buy a couple of sweet, buttery croissants on my way in anticipation of seeing my friend, and as I near the café, I can make out his distinctive form sitting at his favourite table. As usual, he is the picture of elegance, dressed in a white linen shirt and black linen trousers, all styled by Armani, of course. He is reading a newspaper, but as I approach he folds it and lays it on the table.

Standing to greet me, he bends down, kisses me on both cheeks and says, "Hello, darling girl, how are you? Will you join me for coffee?"

Before I can answer, he beckons the waitress and orders two 'grand café cremes'. "Of course, you'll join me," he says, and he pulls out the chair opposite him for me to sit down.

When the coffee arrives, we munch on our croissants and exchange the usual pleasantries before engaging in more serious conversation.

"I've heard about the two murders," Byron says. "I think everyone's heard by now, thanks to that journalist fellow, Junot."

"By tomorrow it will be all over the nationals," I reply, miserably. "A double murder is too big a story to keep quiet for long. I'm still trying to contact other potential victims to warn them of the danger they may be in, but it's difficult to find them. We know where Valentin Foret is supposed to be. He worked at the home. He's at some sort of retreat in Spain, but we haven't been able to speak to him yet. And one of my officers is contacting the church in St Jean, where Pere Gregory is due to take mass tomorrow. He was the spiritual leader for the residents. Dupont, the builder, who was on the board of directors, has moved to Canada to live with his son. We have no idea where Matthew Bryce, another board member, is. Perhaps you know him, he's English, but he's lived in France for over thirty years. I believe he taught English as a second language. Then there's our mayor, Francis. He was also on the board of directors. I'm going to try to speak to him, but there are other issues I must deal with regarding him. So, I have to tread carefully."

"My, my, no wonder you look troubled, dear girl," he replies. "That covers the potential victims, but what about potential suspects?"

"I haven't got a clue. We're still trying to locate the records, but they may give us nothing. They might not even exist. What I really need is a list of the residents and details of their families. I've spoken to one man whose cousin was a resident. He told me that the place was a hellhole and the boys who lived there suffered terrible abuse. He said he'd heard that one boy died and another committed suicide."

"If that's true, then the people who ran the place created their own potential murderer. Some might say 'what goes around comes around'. As Marjorie and Francis are our friends, I think you should speak to them immediately, and perhaps offer him some form of protection. He is the most senior politician we have in this town. It simply wouldn't do to let our mayor be murdered without trying to help him, when you know the potential danger he faces. It would not show you in a very good light. You mentioned another complication regarding Francis. I take it the complication is Monique? Don't let that situation colour your view of him. He is still a potential victim and he is still the mayor. You have to be seen to care about his safety, but of course, you can't possibly protect him 24/7."

As usual, Byron has managed to give me good advice. The way I conduct myself, must be exemplary. My position relies on how I am viewed by the people of this town, and I cannot not let them or myself down. So, after leaving Byron's company, I telephone Francis and arrange to meet him at his home.

Chapter 11

When I ring the bell Francis answers.

"Is Marjorie out?" I ask when I enter the wide hallway.

"Yes, she's out. Actually, she's at your house, visiting Patricia. I thought you'd know that, but then I guess not. Even you can't always know everything."

He seems tetchy, irritated by being in my company.

"I've been expecting you to call for a chat, Danielle. I just wasn't sure when, but it's better sooner than later. Before you begin an embarrassing conversation, I'd just like to say that Marjorie is aware of my girlfriend, Monique. I've been seeing her for some time, and now she's working for me as my P.A., but that's because she's good at the job, not because she's my girlfriend. And besides, it's nobody's business what I get up to in my private life as long as I do my job." he snaps.

His attitude is very confrontational.

"Do you really believe that to be true? Are you so very naïve, Francis?" I reply. "Having an affair is bad enough given your position, but to flaunt your mistress in public and in your office, is unacceptable. How uncomfortable do you think your other employees must feel having to interact with her. And what about the people of the town, your voters. How do you think they'll see it? If forced to choose between you or Marjorie, where do you think their loyalties will lie? With you and your sleazy affair, or with Marjorie, your long-suffering and thoroughly decent wife? And what about your children? They must be dreading their friends finding out in case they're ridiculed. I can just imagine the taunts and teasing. Of course, they'll defend their mother. Then where will that leave you? There's an election next year; this affair could very well cost you your job." I couldn't help the outburst. I am raging with him, but must stop to draw breath.

"You seem to forget, Danielle, I've served three terms in office. Whatever happens, I'll have a pension for life. My children are nearly grown up. They'll just have to get over it and mind their own business. I've fallen in love with Monique and she loves me. I'll sort things out for Marjorie, she'll want for nothing."

"So, you're planning to separate from your loyal, loving wife of many years, for a girl half your age. You're being ridiculous, Francis. When exactly are you planning for this separation to occur?"

"Nothing is going to happen until after next year's election. I do intend to stand again, and I think there's a very good chance I'll be re-elected. People will get used to seeing me with Monique. I certainly won't do anything drastic before the vote that might compromise my chances."

"What a thoroughly selfish man you are," I say. "As it happens, I didn't come here to talk to you about any of this, but I'm pleased it's out in the open. I came here to try to save your life."

I calmly explain to Francis the real reason I'm here. I tell him about the two murders and the danger he may be in.

"The whole thing is crazy," he protests. "I didn't have anything to do with that home. I only visited it once a year for the annual board meeting. I was simply an official to be named on the legal documents. It didn't even have to be me, it could have been anyone, a notaire perhaps, a doctor or even the chief of police. No-one in their right mind would connect me to any suspected wrongdoing at that place."

"That's all very well, Frances, but it wasn't a notaire or a doctor or me. It was you, and this killer is not in his right mind, otherwise we wouldn't already have two dead bodies."

I give him a moment to digest what I've said before continuing.

"As the chief of police, it is my duty to protect you. You're a senior government official. I can't have some maniac bumping you off. As it's a quiet time of year, and as I have a full complement of staff as well as trainees, I propose to assign one of my junior officers to shadow you. We must endeavour to keep you safe until this madman is caught."

Francis' face is scarlet. "Oh, you'd love that," he splutters. "Have me followed day and night, then report back to Marjorie. You must think I was born yesterday! Well I refuse your protection. Do you hear me? I refuse. I'll sign anything you want to absolve you of your responsibilities, but I will not be followed, not by you or anyone."

What an absolute fool he is, I think, but so be it.

"I'll go into the office right now," I say. "If I bring a paper for you to sign within an hour, will you still be here?"

He glances at his watch. "Make it fifty minutes and I'll still be here, after that I'll be out."

"Okay, Francis, fifty minutes it is," I say. Then I leave his house without saying goodbye.

On the way back to the office, I telephone Marie-Therese. "I know you are off duty," I say, "But are you available to accompany me to the mayor's home to witness a signature on a document? It will take less than an hour in total."

"Of course, Boss, just give me the address and tell me when to meet you. Thank you for the opportunity. I appreciate you giving me the extra experience."

I find myself smiling. Gosh she's keen. I tell her the arrangements then briefly inform her what it's about.

"Mon Dieu, Boss. Why is the man being so stupid? He is at risk. He could be murdered. Why refuse help," she asks.

"I don't know," I lie. "Male pride, I suppose," I add.

Forty minutes later I am back at the house. Marie-Therese is already waiting in her car outside. We walk up the pathway together and I ring the bell.

"What's this, reinforcements?" Francis sneers, nodding at Marie-Therese.

We follow him into the dining-room so he can sit at the table while signing the document I've produced.

"Marie-Therese is here to witness your signature. I don't want you coming back to complain after you're murdered," I joke.

Francis scowls at me then scratches his signature without even reading the page.

"Won't you re-consider, sir," Marie-Therese says. "You could be in real danger."

"Boff!" he exclaims. "Just witness my signature then you can both leave."

She quickly signs and within a couple of minutes we are out of the door, having been unceremoniously ejected.

"Well, we gave him every opportunity," I say, when we are back at her car. "Some people just won't accept help. Thanks for your assistance. I'll see you in work on Monday. Come in an hour later to make up for today."

She tries to argue saying she was happy to help, but I insist. It's easier and suits me better than paying her overtime.

Good job well done, I think. Time to go home.

Chapter 12

On Sunday I receive a call from Cedric. It seems he drew the short straw and had to attend the mass at St Jean this morning to speak to Pere Gregory. Although when he arrived, he discovered that the priest hadn't turned up. When he tells me this a chill runs down my spine. Cedric says he's called another cop for support because he's going to check the priest's home. I dread to think what he'll find. Still, at this stage, there's nothing I can do but wait.

Patricia and I continue our lunch in the garden as it's a glorious day. I tell her all about my meeting with Francis and she's very concerned.

"So, Marjorie is right. He is planning to divorce her. What a bastard! We must do something. We can't have Marjorie abandoned and shamed. It would destroy her to have to rely on Frances and his whore for money."

Patricia begins to cry, "I'm so upset," she says. "How can he do this to her. How can he hurt our friend? Where is his conscience? All she's ever done is love him and support him. He's a bastard, a rotten bastard. I hope he becomes impotent. If he was my husband I'd cut his manhood off."

"Remind me never to upset you," I reply. "You're fierce when you're angry."

"We would never hurt each other. Our love is real and honest. Francis is a snivelling rat."

"I didn't know rats snivel," I say, smiling.

She returns my smile, "In my world, if they're called Francis, they do," she replies.

We have just finished eating when Cedric calls again.

"I'm at Pere Gregory's home in Ceret," he says. "He lives here with his house-keeper. She says that she saw him get into his car with a young man and drive off. She thought they were going to the church together, but of course, I know he didn't turn up. What do you want me to do, Boss?"

My mind is racing, has Pere Gregory been abducted? Am I about to have another corpse on my hands?

"Give me the address and stay there. Don't let the housekeeper leave. I'll be with you soon."

"I'm with Officer Bernard, Boss. Do you want him to stay here too, or will I send him back to the church to try to speak to the other priest?"

"Church will be finished now," I reply. "There will be nobody there. Ask Bernard to try to find out who the other priest is and get an address and phone number for him. Also details of anyone who attends the church regularly who might know something about Pere Gregory."

"According to Gregory's housekeeper, he's mostly in retirement and only takes mass from time to time at various churches in the region. He attends as a guest, has lunch, gives a talk, mixes with the congregation, that sort of thing. She says he's very sociable. She thought nothing of it when the young man got into the car with him. It seems he often gives lifts to people."

"Well let's hope we're panicking over nothing," I reply. "But if that's the case, why didn't he turn up this morning and where on earth is he?"

"Yes, indeed, Boss, that's the million-dollar question. I'll wait for you here then. The housekeeper's making us some coffee and sandwiches. She looks about a hundred years old and has a slight steering problem with her walking, a bit wobbly on her legs, but this house is spotless and tidy. She told me she's lived here with the priest for twenty years, so she should know his acquaintances and that might help us."

"Problem?" Patricia asks when I end the call.

"I'm afraid so," I reply. "A priest has gone missing, and not just any priest, but the one who's connected to my investigation. I have to go through to Ceret."

"Oh, darling, what a shame. Just when we'd planned to have a lazy day in the garden."

"Hold that thought, Patricia," I reply. "This might not take very long. I'm sure there will be a simple explanation and he'll turn up. I'm just worrying because of the recent murders. One murder is unusual, two that are connected, extremely rare, I don't want there to be a third. Not on my watch. I'm just panicking because everything is moving so quickly. I feel as if we're constantly playing catch-up."

"Do you think I should invite Marjorie over for coffee while you're out?" Patricia asks. "She's probably on her own. Her children will no doubt be with their friends and Francis will be with his whore. She might be finding her life very lonely, these days. It would suit Francis to have her stuck at home. Out of sight out of mind."

"It's kind of you to think of her," I reply. "But do you really want to spend your lazy Sunday listening to her problems? I know I wouldn't. I'm forced to listen to other people's moans all the time. You must decide for yourself what you want to do, but remember, I might be gone for a few hours and you'll be stuck with her on your own. You can hardly chuck her out once she's here."

She ponders, "You're right," she says. "I'll call her and suggest we meet for coffee in town instead. Then if I've had enough, I can leave. Telephone me when you're heading home and I'll meet you back here. We might still be able to have some time to laze in the sun."

My selfishness has won over her kindness. But I don't feel guilty, not one little bit.

* * *

When I arrive at the address in Ceret, the door is opened by a tiny, cadaverous looking woman. She invites me in, then I follow her down a dark hallway into an even darker room. Cedric is sitting at a dining table which is covered in a crisp, white, cotton tablecloth. He's munching his way through a plate of delicious looking sandwiches, but stands when I approach. The room is filled with the scent of rich, black coffee, and when I'm offered a cup, I happily accept.

Cedric introduces us, "This lady is Madame Ohms," he says. "Madame, this lady is my, boss."

Madame Ohms looks nervous.

"Call me Danielle," I say, offering her my hand to shake.

"Danielle," she repeats looking slightly more relaxed. People in authority frighten her, I think. Not uncommon with her generation. My friendly approach helps.

"I've told your officer all I know," she says. "Which is very little, I'm afraid. I thought nothing of it, when Pere Gregory gave the young man a lift. I hope he's all right."

"Can you describe the man?" I ask.

"He was fairly young, maybe about thirty or forty. And quite tall. Taller than you but much smaller than the officer here, and very skinny. He looked as if his mother didn't feed him properly. His hair needed cutting, it was long and straggly, and he seemed sort of twitchy, nervous maybe. I'm sorry, but that's all I remember. I only saw him for a minute or two."

She's described a man of average height, wide age range, but not particularly young. Skinny and twitchy with straggly hair – a junkie, perhaps, I ponder. It's not a lot to go on.

"How was he dressed?" I ask.

"Like a tramp," she says full of indignation. Imagine getting into a priest's car shabbily dressed. I don't think jeans and a denim jacket are suitable attire for church. I think it's very disrespectful, but then, I suppose lots of young people dress that way nowadays."

"Did you notice if he was he carrying anything?"

"Yes, he had a holdall. It was slung over his shoulder. He put it onto the back seat of the car before he got into the front. There is one further thing you should know," she says, staring at me earnestly. "For Pere Gregory to miss attending mass without informing anyone, means that something urgent and very important must have turned up. He has lovely manners and he wouldn't let anyone down if he could possibly help it."

She's just voiced my concerns.

"Does he have a mobile phone?" Cedric asks.

Good point, I think, I nearly forgot to ask.

"Yes, I'll give you his number."

She reels it off and I put it into my phone.

"Have you tried to call him?"

She looks down at her feet, "No, I didn't like to disturb him."

The man might be being murdered and she doesn't want to disturb him, I think. I shake my head with disbelief.

"You should have tried this number earlier," I say to Cedric. "It might have saved me a trip and us all a lot of time."

"Sorry, Boss," he replies sheepishly. "I've only just thought of it."

"I took it for granted that a telephone call was the first thing you'd have tried," I lie. The truth is, if Cedric hadn't mentioned it, I wouldn't have thought of it either. Sometimes the obvious isn't obvious enough.

I call the number and we all turn towards the ringing phone which is on the cabinet beside the window.

"I guess he forgot his phone. Perhaps that's why he didn't call to cancel his engagement at the church," I say.

There is nothing more we can ask Madame Ohms, so we say our goodbyes and leave the house.

"What now?" Cedric asks.

And I don't really know what to tell him.

Chapter 13

We spend most of the day searching, speaking to people, making telephone calls, just stopping short of scrambling the helicopter to look for Pere Gregory's car, then we receive a call from Bernard.

"Hello, Boss," he says, "I know where the elusive priest is. A hospital social worker has just phoned me to tell me that Pere Gregory is in Perpignan. It seems he's been visiting a man who's in a long-term coma, at the request of someone who said he was a relative. He's still there. Do you want me to go and speak to him?"

"Thanks, Bernard, but no. You've done enough. I'll talk to him. I must warn him to be vigilant because he may be in danger. You go home and see if you can spend a little time with your family. I've got no chance today. So, why should we both suffer? Cedric is with me and we'll see this job through."

I end the call and Cedric and I make our way to the hospital.

"Something doesn't seem right, Boss," he says. "Why the urgency to see a priest, if this man's been in a coma for a long time? And why approach him at his car, instead of knocking on his door or phoning to make an appointment? Something doesn't add up. And who is this scruffy man? We must find out. For all we know he may have been involved in the previous murders. Perhaps this was a trial run at abducting the priest."

"You're right, Cedric. It's all very odd. If we're lucky, the man will still be with Pere Gregory. Phone the hospital and have them keep the priest there. Tell them it's vital we speak to him, and that for his own safety, he must not be allowed to leave. If the other man is with him, ask the hospital security guard to detain him. If he's innocent, he won't mind waiting twenty minutes until we arrive, and if he's not, we'll have him."

We get to the hospital quickly as the traffic is light, but finding the department is a nightmare. Eventually, we are guided to a small, dimly lit ward at the farthest point of the building. There is nothing uplifting or inspiring about the place; it feels like a dying room. I am sure that people only depart from here in a box. Pere Gregory is pacing the floor. He looks upset and agitated. He grabs my arm in both his hands when I introduce myself.

"I don't understand what's going on," he says. "The man told me it was an emergency. He said his father was dying and there was no-one to administer the last rites. Now the hospital social worker has told me that he is not dying, but in a coma. And she said that the man who led me here is not known to her. She's never seen him before. They think he might be a mental patient. How can that be? The man knew my name. He knew where I lived."

I sit Pere Gregory down in a small waiting room and tell him about Henri and Roland. His face pales and he looks as though he might faint.

"I'd heard that Henri was dead, but I didn't know he'd been murdered. And now you say Roland has been killed as well. Do you think I've just had a lucky escape?" he asks.

"I simply don't know," I reply honestly. "Maybe the man who asked you here knows the coma patient. Perhaps he wanted to give him comfort by bringing you to pray for him. What did he tell you about himself? Did he tell you his name?"

"All he said was that his name was Luke and his father, the patient, is Charles Mayer."

"And is the man in the bed Charles Mayer?" I ask.

"Yes, according to his notes, he is."

"Did you know Monsieur Mayer previously. Have you any connection to him?"

"No, none. The nurse told me he's only been in this region for about a year. He was visiting from Paris and suffered a head trauma. That's how he ended up here."

"When did you realise something was wrong?"

"When a nurse came into the room to ask who we were and why we were here. Luke, the young man, ran from the room and disappeared. The hospital security guard looked but couldn't find him. As you can imagine officer, I am very upset. I don't really understand any of this."

He is elderly and stooped and he seems completely bewildered. Seeing him like this, it is easy to forget that this man might be a sadistic monster who tortured children.

"My officer will take a statement from you, Pere Gregory. We'll get you some coffee, and then, if you don't feel like driving, he will take you home in your car and I'll follow in mine. The chances are the hospital is correct and the man might simply have mental health issues. You'll probably never hear from him again. But, just in case, until the murderer is apprehended, you should be extra vigilant. Make sure you keep your doors locked and don't take any unnecessary risks. If you are visiting a parishioner, don't go alone, take someone with you."

"But officer," he protests, "I'm a man of the cloth, a priest, God will protect me. If the man I met today is a cold-blooded killer, I've survived. Perhaps he wanted to confess his sins to me, but didn't know how to begin. I cannot separate myself from the people who need me. I represent God."

What a stupid, arrogant fool, I think. One minute he's scared and bewildered and the next he's spouting pious rubbish. Oh, well, I've tried my best. Let's hope God is on top form, because the murderer certainly is.

We take his statement and see him home. Then I drive Cedric to his car and we say our goodbyes. By the time I arrive back, it is after nine. Patricia has a meal ready for me. She quickly reheats it in the microwave and I wolf it down with half of a bottle of robust red wine. It's such a relief to be here, safe in my home, with everyone and everything I love. It is calm here. I can lock the door and shut out the mayhem and madness of the world outside.

* * *

The next day dawns and I'm up with the lark. I've slept well, all things considered. We're no further on in tracking down the killer, but at least we don't have another victim. I am feeling quite cheerful until I reach the office and Inspector Gerard, my superior from Perpignan, is waiting outside.

"Danielle," he says. "Let's go inside. We need to talk."

I unlock the door. I'm concerned that he's here and has arrived with no warning. I wonder if I'm in trouble. Marie-Therese enters at my back. She's early, thank goodness.

"Look after the office," I say, and Gerard accompanies me to my room.

When we are seated with coffee, he produces a newspaper from his briefcase.

"Have you seen this?" he asks pointing to an article on the front page.

'Crazed killer on the loose', it states. 'Two men murdered', is the subtext. The story has been accredited to Junot.

"Oh, merde," I sigh. "I had no idea he'd managed to sell the story to a national."

"Prepare to be descended on from a great height," Gerard says. "Everyone and their trained monkeys will arrive. A double homicide is such a rare occurrence, thank God, that the media will have a field day. Particularly with the focus of attention being a home for delinquents. I'm sending you extra officers. You won't be able to cope otherwise. Are you any closer to finding the culprit? I imagine it's a bit like finding a needle in a haystack."

"We have so little information, Sir," I reply. "If we can find the records of the residents, we'll be able to investigate them. I have drawn up a list of everyone who was involved with the home and we're working our way through that. Our mayor, who was on the board of directors, has refused our protection. We had an incident yesterday with the priest who oversaw the spiritual needs of the residents. It seems he has little concern for his safety. He assured me that God will protect him. My officers are diligent and hardworking, but as you rightly say, we have little to go on, and I'd value any advice you can give me."

He rubs his chin with his hand. "Take on the media, Danielle. You go to them. That way you can control what they report. Call a press conference and ask for their help. Get them to ask anyone who was resident in the home, or anyone else who has information, to come forward. That will cut out this fellow, Junot. His personal spin on the reporting is the danger, because he can challenge what you do or say. If the press has only his story, they could hang you out to dry. As I said, I'll send you extra officers to cope with the volume of work and I'll send you a press officer to assist you with the media."

I think about what he's said and it terrifies me, but he's right. I must deal with this situation head on. The story is already out there.

"Thank you, sir," I reply.

He stands and is about to leave, then says, "Use the media, Danielle. This will put you in the spotlight, but only good can come of it. You'll be viewed as an intrepid, law enforcement officer, fighting evil, searching for a crazed killer. Whether you catch the bastard or not, the public will be behind you all the way. Most people these days see life as a graphic novel or a computer game. They can no longer think for themselves. The longer you can milk the limelight, the more popular you'll become. And, if you do get your killer, you'll be a super hero. I don't care if you take him dead or alive. Dead costs the taxpayer less," he says, and gives me a wry smile.

"And would you like to take part in this media circus?" I offer.

"No thank you, Danielle, when you become a superhero, I'll make an appearance. I'll give you a commendation and a monetary bonus for your achievement. You know the drill. We've been here before. You do the work, I take some of the credit and reward you handsomely. Don't let me down and everybody wins."

He gives me a limp, greasy handshake and he's on his way.

Yes, I think to myself, we have been here before. I'm out on a limb, taking all the risks, and he sits in his comfy office and waits for the outcome. If I'm successful, he takes the credit and, if the unthinkable happens and I fail, he has someone to blame.

How I despise the man.

Chapter 14

By late afternoon, it feels as if the office is under siege - two of my tallest officers guard the door to stop journalists from entering. After much thought about what I will say, I telephone the Mairie and book a room for tomorrow at 10am, then I step outside to face the wolves. Immediately I'm out of the door, I'm bombarded with voices and blinded by flashing cameras.

"Mesdames et Messieurs," I shout over the rabble. "Please, be quiet and let me speak or we'll get nowhere."

A hush falls over the crowd.

"If you will be good enough to attend a public meeting tomorrow morning at 10am at the Mairie, I will be making a statement about the terrible events that have recently taken place in this region. You will be expected to conduct yourselves in an orderly and polite manner. To ask a question, you must hold up your hand, and when invited, you will state your name and the newspaper you represent. I will answer one question and only one question from each newspaper, so think carefully about what you want to ask me. Once I have given the statement and answered questions, the hall will be emptied. If after this, you harass me or my staff or any member of the public – you will be arrested for breaching the peace. Do I make myself clear?"

There are rumblings of dissent, but nobody is brave enough to speak out.

"Right," I say. "Please now be on your way. Go to your hotels, or wherever else you are staying, and I'll see you all tomorrow."

Nobody makes a move.

"You heard the chief, get going," Paul shouts, "unless anyone wants to spend the night in a cell."

The crowd reluctantly disperses amidst much muttering, and I and my fellow officers return inside.

"You were magnificent, Boss!" Paul exclaims. "Absolutely magnificent."

"You didn't do too badly, yourself," I reply.

Then I address all the officers present, "We must now get on the phones and warn everyone who is involved with this that the circus is in town. For their own protection, we must ask them to make no comments. People like the Poullets, Georges Michel, Pere Gregory and his housekeeper, Monsieur and Madame le mayor. Anyone who you think the press will try to contact. Extra officers are being drafted in to help us and we are also being given a press officer, whatever that might be. But for the time being, we are on our own and we must be strong. Any sign of weakness and they'll devour us like a pack of wild dogs."

I pause and look each of them in the eye. "Are you ready, children," I say.

The resounding cheering and applause tells me they are.

When we are finished for the day and lock up the office, I am pleased to see that there are no journalists hanging around to waylay my staff. I guess they got the message, I think. If only they knew how much they terrify me. The thought has no sooner left my head, when I am confronted by Junot in the car park. I walk swiftly past him.

"Danielle, Danielle," he calls, scurrying after me. "Wait up, wait up, I've something to tell you. I have information you'll want to hear."

"I don't think so, Junot," I reply, but I give him the benefit of the doubt and allow him to catch up with me. "Well, what do you have to tell me?" I ask. "Make it quick, Junot, it's been a long day," I snap.

"Can we go somewhere and sit down, please, Danielle. I too have had a long day."

His face looks strained and his pallor is grey. I can't bear the man, but I can see that he's tired and I relent.

"Come over to my car, we'll sit there," I offer. "But I don't have much time," I add.

When we are seated he begins.

"When you visited the hospital in Perpignan to fetch Pere Gregory you saw the man who's in a coma, Charles Mayer. You were told that he'd come to the area about a year ago and suffered a head trauma. Now he's little more than a vegetable."

"Are you going to tell me something I don't know, Junot, or are we wasting our time here?"

"Patience, Danielle, I'm getting there," he replies. "Didn't you wonder why Pere Gregory had been led to that particular patient?" He pauses for effect, and this time I don't interrupt him. "Charles Mayer has no obvious connection to this region, but his ex-wife has. She came to Ceret from Paris when they divorced because she had a job offer. She brought her youngest son, who was a teenager at the time, with her. The older son was already an adult and working in Paris, so he stayed with his father. The youngest son was always in trouble and he ended up being sent to the home. After being there for a year, he committed suicide."

I am totally stunned. "How did you discover this?" I ask. I really want to add, 'when we did not', but say nothing more.

"From the records of the home," he replies.

"We have been searching for those records. How did you get hold of them?" I ask.

"From Pere Gregory. He has all the records and some letters too. He telephoned me, wanting me to try to find the man who led him to the hospital. He told me the man was very troubled and needed to confess his sins. He said that if I could find him, then he could save his mortal soul. I think he believes that this man is the murderer. When I left Pere Gregory, he said he was going to have a sketch artist draw an impression of him for me, so I can put it in a newspaper. Then we can ask the public for assistance. The strange thing is, I had previously tried asking the mayor about records from the home, but he said he couldn't help me as he knew nothing about them. It was sheer luck that the priest contacted me, or I'd never have discovered them. Up until then, I didn't even know if any existed. Going to speak to him was a long shot that paid off. Once he showed me them, I simply searched for the name, Mayer. I found it almost immediately, in a letter. I promised Pere Gregory I wouldn't go to the police, but that I'd return in a couple of days to pick up the sketch. He doesn't want you to try to stop him. Silly old man could get himself killed."

I find myself having a new respect for Junot. "You lied to a priest," I say. "You'll burn in hell."

He laughs then continues. "The ex-wife, Angela, still lives in the region, in a suburb of Perpignan, and she still uses the surname, Mayer. It took me quite a while and many phone calls to people with that name, but I eventually found her. Unfortunately, she's an alcoholic and she's rarely sober, but she told me what I needed to know. Her oldest son, Luke, came back from Paris. He is now thirty-two and a junkie, he was ten years older than the brother, Christian. The whole family has problems. She said that her son never got over his brother's death and neither did she. She's a very angry woman, very bitter. I think you should try to discover how Charles Mayer received his head trauma, because it may be connected to the murders."

"Why have you given me this information, Junot?" I ask. I'm suspicious. "What do you want in return?"

"I work as a journalist for a living. Often, it's hard to make ends meet. Now that I've sold a story to a national newspaper, they'll take more work from me. If you can give me anything before the other papers get it, then I'll have a chance. I'm always looking for a scoop. Or perhaps you can suggest a different angle on a story, or inside information to flesh out a story, that the others don't know. I'll take anything you can offer me."

I hadn't thought about Junot having to earn his daily bread. He was always just an annoyance as far as I was concerned.

"I'll do my best to help you," I say. "But I expect nothing less from you," I add.

"Deal," he says grinning, and he offers me his hand to shake.

I take his hand, "Deal," I agree.

Before we part company, he gives me all the contact details he has for the Mayer family. And now that I also know where the records are it will save Marie-Therese hours of work trawling through the archives of the Mairie. So, the priest didn't tell us the whole truth, I think; he led us to believe that Valentin Foret was the record keeper, and yet, he is the one with the paperwork we need. Junot is right, I must find out more about how Charles Mayer received his head injury. Could he have been the murderer's first intended victim?

Not long after I get home, I practically fall into bed with exhaustion. I've barely managed to eat my dinner and haven't had much conversation with Patricia. Dealing with the media has drained me and I must rise early tomorrow to produce my statement for the meeting. I noticed that Patricia had been holding a couple of booklets in her hand when I first arrived home, but she placed them under a cookery book on the window ledge when she saw how tired I was. I'm curious to know what they are, but it can't be anything urgent or important or she would have said something.

I toss and turn for a couple of hours, nodding off for only ten minutes at a time, before I give up and go downstairs. Once there, I sit at the kitchen table and within a short time, I manage to scribble down my statement to read to the media. It's such a relief to have it ready that I return to my bed and fall asleep as soon as my head hits the pillow.

The next day dawns and my meeting goes well. Only a few journalists attend along with a smattering of townspeople whose curiosity has got the better of them. I stand at the front of the room with two of my officers, while a further two guard the door. After I read my statement, the questions are mostly straightforward and easily answered, but there is one I choose not to give an opinion on as it's a medical question, so I simply say, 'no comment'. In just over an hour I am back at the office.

The rest of the day passes in a blur of confusion and wasted effort. There are far too many people in the office all attempting to be involved in the same jobs. Pere Gregory's housekeeper advises us that he'll be out all day as he's visiting a chapel in Girona, so there's no chance of getting the records until tomorrow. Valentin Foret has yet to appear although Matthew Bryce, one of the men who was on the board of directors, has been reached by phone. He has moved away to live with his girlfriend in Provence. We tell him about what has happened here, but he seems unconcerned.

Once again, I return home exhausted and retire early.

Chapter 15

When I wake the next morning it is very early, barely daybreak, but I feel rested. I make myself coffee and check out the publications that Patricia placed under the cookery book. They are all about becoming a foster parent. After I glance at them, I replace them under the book. I know Patricia would like a child in our lives, but I am not interested. We both have work commitments that take up much of our time. If one of us became pregnant then we'd have to deal with the consequences, but it's unlikely to happen. Patricia is a lesbian and although it's possible for her to get pregnant with a donor, she is very unlikely to go down that route, no matter how desperate for a child she becomes. Neither of us is in a relationship, and although we love each other, we are not a couple. The thought of an ever-changing parade of children taking over my home, my sanctuary, doesn't bear thinking about. I think Patricia's dream is much different from the reality, but then life's often like that.

When she comes into the kitchen for breakfast, I decide to broach the subject. I don't want to be put on the spot, so I intend to get my views across first.

"I don't know how that woman, Beatrix, manages with all the children she's been involved with," I begin. "It's clear she has little time for other commitments. As she said, it's her career choice, but still, it must restrict her life. Imagine having to plan holidays in between different children coming and going, because they can't stay overnight anywhere but the foster home. I would hate not being able to be spontaneous, wouldn't you?"

"I haven't really thought much about it," she replies, but I see from her downcast look, that's she's thought of nothing else, and she's disappointed by what I've said.

"Do you have time to come home for lunch?" she asks, changing the subject. "Marjorie is coming over."

"Sorry, darling, I'm too busy. We're surrounded by journalists because of the murders, and we still must take care of the day to day problems that crop up, so my day will be solid work. The extra staff drafted in are all very well, but I've nowhere to put them, the office is small. The press officer has been useful, but he's leaving us tomorrow. He says most of the journalists will follow him back to Perpignan because they now realise nobody, other than he, will speak to them. I do hope he's right. Their presence is claustrophobic."

She seems deep in thought for a few moments, then says, "You're right, we do work hard. I suppose being a foster carer should only be considered as a full-time job. It would never suit us, but I'd love to find a way to spend some time with children. I find them so amusing. It's just a pity we don't have any nieces or nephews."

"Why don't you contact the primary school," I suggest. "Perhaps from time to time they need volunteers to help with things like school trips or events."

Her face lights up. "That's a great idea, Danielle. There are also clubs like the scouts. They might need helpers. I'll investigate the possibilities. Thanks for the suggestion."

I'm pleased with myself. Problem averted, I think. Sometimes the voice of common sense must be selfish.

When I get into the office it's bedlam once again; there are people everywhere, all of them cops. Nobody knows what to do or where to put themselves. I can stand it no longer. We cannot work like this. Time to get back to normal, to regain control.

Firstly, I go outside to the waiting journalists, only three are there this morning, thank God.

I say, "You must move away from the doorway. The public is intimidated by your presence. The press officer is returning to Perpignan tomorrow. He is the only person who can tell you anything. The rest of the journalists have already left. They've gone to the central police office there."

It's a lie, I have no idea where the other journalists have gone, or indeed, if they have left. But it'll do for now. My words have the desired effect, and within a couple of minutes they move away.

Then I call Gerard and tell him I'm returning the extra staff. He says I can keep them for a few days more if I want. I tell him, 'thanks, but no thanks.' I have no room for them to work here, and nothing for them to do. Now that the records of the home have been located, my own staff can go through them. I'd prefer it that way. I want everything within my control. I don't want outsiders knowing where we are with this investigation. I don't want these random cops reporting back to Gerard. I'll give him information when I'm good and ready.

I instruct Cedric and Bernard to go to Pere Gregory's home and pick up the records.

"Don't take any nonsense from him," I say. "Warn him not to speak to the press. Tell him we have an officer who deals with that, and give Pere Gregory his contact number. Let him think that anything he says, might put the man he seeks, in danger. He might have no worries about his own safety, but I don't think he'll risk the man's. It's too late to completely warn him off, of course, because he's already spoken to Junot, but he doesn't know that we know about their conversation."

After all the balls are set in motion and calm begins to return, I telephone Junot for an update. He tells me he's had no further calls from Pere Gregory.

"The priest's a bit doddery, Danielle," he says. "It's all very well him telling me he's going to engage a sketch artist, but where is he going to find one? I think he got a bit carried away with himself, and when he's calmer, he'll let this stupid notion drop. Although he doesn't want to admit it, he got a fright the other day. He was vulnerable and easily led. Once he gets off his high horse, he'll realise that he's only human, even with God's help."

"I hope you're right, Junot," I reply. "I don't want the silly, old fool meddling."

I tell him the other journalists are leaving, following the press officer to Perpignan.

"Do you think I should go with them?" he asks.

"No, my advice is stay here. I'll get any breaking news first, and I'll tell you long before it goes to Perpignan. We have a deal. And I always honour my promises."

Junot is delighted, he offers to buy me coffee.

"Let's get one thing straight, Junot," I say. "We will work together because we have an arrangement, but don't be mistaken, we are not friends. I don't even like you."

I hear him laughing as he hangs up the phone and I find myself smiling too.

* * *

We don't have time for a proper lunch break, so Marie-Therese picks up sandwiches for herself, Paul and me. We eat quickly then I drive us all through to Perpignan. It's vital we locate Luke Mayer, and the only address we have for the family is his mother's apartment. She lives in a poor part of town inhabited by many foreigners, mostly asylum seekers and refugees. The streets are full of children who look grubby and unkempt, with tangled hair and runny noses. I think a solid meal wouldn't go amiss.

"This is a terrible place," Marie-Therese says, as she dodges around litter and dog dirt.

"Welcome to the real world," Paul replies.

Some parts are more real than others, I think. Finally, in the middle of a dingy road, we locate the apartment of Angela Meyer. We enter the dark hallway, littered with used needles and rubbish, with trepidation. I bang on the door. Marie-Therese has her hand on her baton, and I know she's scared. Paul and I are apprehensive too as we don't know what to expect. I hear a shuffling behind the door; it opens a crack and a haggard looking woman peers out. Her hair is so thin, I can see her scalp and her face is pockmarked.

"He's not here and I have no money," she says before I can ask the question.

She's about to shut the door, when Paul places his boot in the opening. "We're the police," he says. "We don't want your money. Open this door and let us in," he commands, and surprisingly, she does.

The inside of the apartment is no better than the outside. It's dirty, litter-strewn and dank.

"We are looking for your son, Luke," I say. "Do you know where he is?"

"He's done nothing wrong," she states. "And he's not here," she repeats.

"He's not in any trouble," Paul says, and Marie-Therese throws me a look because she knows he's lying. "Please just tell us where he hangs out."

She eyes us suspiciously, then says, "Sometimes he begs outside the bus station. He needs to get money for drugs, or he gets ill," she explains. "Please, don't hurt him," she begs. "He's a good boy. It's not his fault. He's a poor soul."

That's the problem with junkies, I think, nothing is ever their fault.

"That place was awful," Marie-Therese says, when we exit the building. "I felt like wiping my feet on the way out, but it's just as bad out here. The smell was the worst thing about it. I didn't know if it was coming from her or the place."

"Probably both," Paul replies.

We are silent as we make our way to the bus station. I am contemplating the vast difference between my life and Angela Mayer's and I suspect my colleagues are too. When we arrive, I see two beggars sitting on the ground outside and one matches Luke's description. As soon as we step from the car, he takes off at speed, running and leaping like a frightened deer. He must have an instinct about cops.

"That's all we need," Paul says, rolling his eyes. "It's twenty-eight degrees today," he adds.

The words are barely out of his mouth, when Marie-Therese takes off in pursuit, baton at the ready.

"Mon Dieu!" Paul exclaims, as we try to follow. "She runs like a greyhound. Just look at her go."

She is weaving and winding her way past pedestrians and cars as we struggle to keep up. Eventually, she and her prey reach the wide square of the Place de la Catalogne. They run in front of a line of cars, which fortunately, are stopped at traffic lights, before Marie-Therese finally catches up with Luke. Then she hits out with her baton and catches him behind the knees, flooring him. He is handcuffed, and she's dragged him to the pavement before we reach them.

We are bent over and gasping for breath, but she's hardly broken into a sweat.

"You didn't tell me you were an Olympic runner," Paul says, his voice full of admiration.

"You're just unfit," she replies. "This washed-up junkie managed to outrun you," she says, pointing to Luke and laughing. "Too much beer and chips, perhaps?" she adds.

"And what about me?" I ask. "Do you think that I also, consume too much beer and chips?"

"No, Boss, not at all. You're just a bit older than me, that's all."

Paul splutters with laughter. "I don't know what's worse, Boss," he says, "Being a fat bastard or an unfit, old bag."

"I am not old," I protest, as we drag our captive back up the hill to my car. "I'm just older than this child. But you're right. You are a bastard to suggest it."

"Whatever you say, Boss," Paul replies, chuckling. "Whatever you say."

We confirm that we have our man then drive back towards the office with Luke and Paul in the back seat. Luke is moaning and protesting.

"I didn't do anything. I'm innocent. Police brutality," he says. "I'll tell your boss, then you'll be in trouble."

"I am the boss," I reply. "Shut your mouth or you'll feel police brutality with the back of my hand," I add.

He begins to sob.

"Oh, good God, stop crying, stupid boy," I say.

"I don't want to die," he wails. "I need a fix. I need a fix, or I'll die. Take me to the hospital. They'll give me something. I'm in pain."

"As soon as you answer my questions, I'll let you go," I say.

"What do you want to know? Ask me now. Soon, I'll be in so much pain I won't be able to talk. Quick, ask me now. I feel sick. I need my poison, or I'll be sick."

He's agitated, and his eyes are wild, darting this way and that. Marie-Therese looks upset and scared.

"Pull in, boss," Paul says. "I don't want him throwing up on me. He doesn't look well."

I'm glad it's Paul sitting beside him and not me. I stop the car at the side of the road, where there's a bus stop with a bench, and we all pile out. Luke falls onto the road, shaking and retching. There is nothing in his stomach to come up but bile. When he finishes being sick, Paul hauls him onto the bench and I question him.

"Why did you murder Henri Boudin and Roland Michel?" I ask.

"Wwhat?" he stammers. "I didn't kill anyone. I'm not violent. No way."

"Why did you take Pere Gregory to see your father? What did you hope to achieve?"

"I wanted him to see what he'd done. He destroyed my family. He beat my little brother so often that he couldn't take any more. Christian killed himself, because he couldn't stand it. He was so desperate and afraid, and it was that bastard's fault. The priest was meant to protect him, and instead he drove him to suicide. But I didn't hurt the old man, I promise you that, I just wanted him to see what he'd done."

He is wracked with sobs. His body is twitching and shaking uncontrollably and I think he might have a fit.

"My mum's an alcoholic, my dad felt so much guilt that he drove into a wall, and I'm a heroin addict. That man destroyed my whole family. I just wanted him to see what he'd done. I just wanted him to see..."

Luke passes out. He slips to the ground, his head rocking, his body fitting.

"Call an ambulance, Paul," I say, as I place him in the recovery position.

Marie-Therese is shocked, her eyes well with tears. "How awful," she says. "I believe him, Boss. Do you think he's telling the truth?"

I rub my hand over my face. "I'm sorry to say, yes, I do. It would have been so easy if he were the killer. But there's no way he could have the strength, and besides, his brain is frazzled from drugs. He couldn't even begin to dream up such a crime."

"Back to the drawing board, then," Paul says. He stares at the twitching young man. "I'm glad we got him out of the car," he adds, dispassionately, "Because he's just peed his pants."

Chapter 16

Even although Luke is not guilty of anything other than lying to the priest about his father's imminent death, catching up with him so quickly made me look good. When I telephone Gerard, he's delighted.

"That was good police work," he says.

"It was mostly down to my latest trainee, Marie-Therese," I reply.

It's nothing for me to give the girl praise. After all, she was the one to apprehend Luke. Paul and I would never have caught up with him. We discuss her progress and I let it be known that I'd like to keep her at my office once she completes her training.

"She sounds like one to watch," Gerard says. "From what you've told me she could be a high flyer like you."

Most senior officers in the force are men, and most of them would choose a man from the list of new recruits for any permanent position in their office. It's difficult for old prejudices to change. So, I doubt I'll be competing for Marie-Therese, even although she will probably be amongst the top qualifiers.

I end the call, then immediately contact Junot to give him the story. He's delighted when I describe the chase and mention Marie-Therese as the arresting officer. And even more delighted when I tell him we sought medical help for Luke.

"He was in a poor state of health and needed care," I say. "So, we didn't bring him to our office for questioning. A sick young man's health is important to the police and must take precedence over everything else."

"Can I use that as a quote?" he asks, excitedly.

"That's why I said it," I reply. "It will give your reader a 'feel good' impression of the police."

"I'll focus my story on the calibre of the people who are joining the police force, and re-enforce that the police are here to help the public, even if they are suspected of a crime. Don't worry, Danielle. You and your team will come out of this article smelling of roses."

"I expect nothing less, Junot. It's nice doing business with you," I add, then end the call.

Giving the article that sort of spin, will draw attention away from the fact that we have nothing on the murders to report.

Somehow, by the time the story reaches the local paper, it is front page news. The headline reads, 'brave female cop saves the day'. Paul guffaws with laughter when he reads it.

"The nationals will soon be asking for your photo," he says to Marie-Therese. "And local people will want your autograph," he adds.

"You're just jealous because you couldn't catch the man, because you're too fat and lazy," she fires back.

Now the rest of the office staff are laughing.

"You tell him, sister," the secretary says and high fives Marie-Therese.

"No fighting children," I say, "We've got work to do. I need a volunteer to help me police the dog show on Sunday."

Every head is down, avoiding the parapet, except Marie-Therese. "I love dogs," she says. "I'll help you, Boss."

"That's why you're in the paper," I say. "You're a star. Take your own car. It's a local venue, they're setting up beside the stables. I'll meet you there at 10 o'clock and I'll buy the lunches. My friend is entering our dog, so I must attend anyway. The rest of you are off the hook."

I return to my room feeling rather pleased with myself. Things are settling back to normal in the office. We now have the records from the home. Bernard and Cedric had rather a hard time extracting them from Pere Gregory. He gave all sorts of excuses why he couldn't give them out, from data protection to betrayal of trust, but none of it was relevant. Apart from the list of residents and the dates they arrived then subsequently left the home, all other records appear to be in code. There are dates, companies, donations, several amounts of money listed, but we can't tell what was money coming in and what was going out. It's clear that this is going to take some time to decipher. When questioned, Pere Gregory said that, he too, didn't understand any of it as Valentin had been the record keeper. He told us that he had merely stored the paperwork after the home closed.

I ask Marie-Therese to concentrate on the boys, their names, previous addresses, why they were placed there, who they befriended, anything that shows a pattern. Most have a series of numbers against their names, some of them are the same and some different, but we have no idea what they stand for. At least, by studying the records, it looks as if we are working on the cases, although we are under no pressure just now as nobody is pressing us for answers. That thought is barely out of my mind when my phone rings.

"Hello, Boss, Doctor Poullet is in the office. He's demanding to speak to you," Paul says.

Merde, I think, I should have known today was too good to be true. "You'd better show him through," I reply. "Then go out and get me some 'pain au chocolate', I need sustenance and something to bribe the old devil with. Bring it straight back here as soon as possible."

Within a couple of minutes, Poullet rolls into the room, wheezing and mopping his brow.

"My wife is driving me mad," he says, as he flops into a chair. "She made me come here to ask you for an update on Saint Henri. I told her you will come to us when you have information. May I sit here for a while? I can't be seen outside, or I'll get an earful from her again."

I'm relieved. He's not after my blood. I tell him about Pere Gregory and the Mayer family and I give him information that wasn't covered by Junot's reporting. He's delighted.

"Thank you, Danielle, now I have something to tell my wife."

Paul arrives with the pastries. He knocks on my door then peers in, hesitantly, holding the bag of pastries in front of him as protection.

"You're meant to wait until you are invited in, after knocking. Where are your manners? We're discussing my personal business," Poullet roars. "Would you like your personal business discussed in front of all and sundry? Would you want me to talk to the baker or the butcher about your boils or piles?"

"Nnno, sorry," Paul stammers. "I don't have boils or piles," he adds, looking at me beseechingly.

"Put the bag on the desk, please," I say.

He places it down and runs from my room, hauling the door shut as he leaves.

"You are a very bad man," I say to Poullet.

"That's why we get on so well," he replies. He is obviously pleased with himself. His wife has bullied him now he has bullied Paul. He then opens the bag, removes a pastry and takes a large bite from it, dropping buttery crumbs over himself and my desk.

"Coffee," he demands. "You know how I like it – two heaped spoons of sugar."

He takes another pastry. He's smiling now. No wonder he's so fat, I think. I don't eat any of the chocolatey treats, watching him has put me off.

Chapter 17

Sunday is a glorious day, and Patricia has been up since dawn preparing for the dog show. I hadn't realised that she'll be taking a small stall to sell her fruit pies. All the money raised is for charity, so I applaud her generosity. She assures me that someone else will man it for part of the day to let her enter Ollee in a competition. However, Crufts, it will not be. Owners and their dogs will be invited to take part in contests to discover who has the biggest or the smallest dog, the one with the waggiest tail, the best rescue dog and the dog who looks most like their owner. There will also be more serious events based on obedience and sheep herding.

Ollee has had a bath in preparation, two in fact, as immediately he was spruced up the first time, he ran into the garden and rolled in something disgusting. To him, it must have smelled like Chanel No5, but to anyone standing beside him, it was eyewatering.

"Thank goodness for tomato ketchup," Patricia says. "It's the only thing that neutralises that awful stink. I think he rolled in fox's droppings. I simply mixed ketchup with some liquid soap and bathed him with it. He's not getting outside again until we can put him straight into the car."

Ollee has the good grace to look ashamed, although I don't think he has any idea of what he's done wrong.

The stables are near enough our home that we can walk there, but with all the stuff we have, I must take the car. However, the proximity will allow me to drink some wine as I'll be able to walk home afterwards, and pick up the car tomorrow. If any emergency occurs, Marie-Therese will have her car and can drive me. That's the beauty about being the boss, I can bend the rules and someone else will be on call to sort things out if required.

When we arrive, the place is buzzing. The organisers and volunteers are milling about: setting up stalls, marking off areas with tape, and their dogs are running around yipping, and sniffing and getting under everyone's feet. It's rather chaotic, but nobody seems to mind. The atmosphere is one of good natured excitement.

Marie-Therese arrives early. She is with her friend, a petite, pretty girl named Elise, and the most enormous dog I've ever seen. "He's a Leonberger," Elise explains.

The dog's head is the size of a beach ball. He looks like a lion and his paws are huge.

"Don't let Arnie jump up to greet you," she warns. "He weighs a ton and he's taller than you. If he puts his paws on your shoulders to give you a hug, he'll flatten you."

I have no doubt what she's said is true, and I have no intention of getting too close to the dog.

"I suppose Arnie is entered into the biggest dog category," I reply.

"Certainly not the dog who looks most like the owner," Marie-Therese says laughing. "Elise is tiny and Arnie, well Arnie is the Arnold Schwarzenegger of the dog world. That's how he got his name."

"I'm sure your dog will win," I say. "I've never seen a beast as big as him."

"Wait until Bruno gets here with Boy, he's an enormous Great Dane. He's even bigger than my friend's donkey. Then there's Tiny, the Mastiff, she belongs to Ian, the Scotsman, and she's a monster of a dog. There are also a couple of working dogs owned by Maurice. They're Pyrenean Mountain dogs and they're big too. Maurice lives high up in the mountain and uses them to round up his sheep and goats, so they're very muscular and strong."

"I had no idea there were so many huge dogs living in the area," I say.

"Yes," Elise replies, "and there are dozens of very tiny dogs as well; so there will certainly be no shortage of entries for the competitions."

I tell Marie-Therese to enjoy her day with her friend, but to meet me at lunchtime so we can all eat together and update each other if there's anything to report. Patricia has packed us a picnic and there'll easily be enough for Elise and five or six other people as well. Obviously, if there is any trouble, we can telephone each other for support. Not that I'm expecting anything to occur.

"Treat it like a paid day off - one of the perks of the job," I suggest, and Marie-Therese is delighted.

The gates open and hundreds of people flock in. I had no idea the event would be so popular. Marjorie approaches and welcomes us with hugs and kisses.

"Francis is opening the show in about five minutes," she says. "Shame they couldn't get anyone better than the mayor to start things off," she adds, her voice full of bitterness.

"Shouldn't you find him?" I ask. I expect her to be on the podium beside him.

"Now why would I want to do that?" she replies. "The bastard can manage without me very well. I'd much rather spend time with my friends."

Patricia and I look at each other, but neither of us says a word. Instead we all make our way to the front of the crowd.

"Let's see him talk his way out of this," Marjorie says. "Let's see him explain why I'm not standing beside him as usual."

She really hates him, I think.

The chairman of the charity gives a speech, and thanks everyone for turning out. "Please spend lots of money at the stalls and games," she says. "Every centime raised will help the charity. Now I'd like to ask our mayor, to step up and officially open the event. He is assisted today by his P.A., Monique." There is a muttering of sound, then silence resumes.

"Hello, everyone," Francis begins. "As Madame Chairperson said, Monique is my new P.A. I've asked Marjorie to step aside from her usual role beside me today, so I can introduce you to Monique. She assists me in the day to day running of the Mairie. Hello, Marjorie," he calls over, waving. "And hello, Danielle. Mesdames et Messieurs, as you can see, we also have our chief of police here, so don't do anything wrong or she'll arrest you." This raises a laugh. The mood is lightened.

Marjorie is shaking with rage, but somehow manages to keep a benign look on her face. Patricia is so incensed, I fear she might attack him.

"How dare he?" she hisses. "Look at the smug bastard. How can he do that to Marjorie?"

"Let it go, Patricia," Marjorie replies. "I caused this by refusing to stand beside him."

"But that whore shouldn't even be here," Patricia protests. "She doesn't even own a dog."

"She doesn't need to," Marjorie replies. "She's a bitch, herself."

We all find ourselves laughing.

"Keep that thought, Marjorie. Stick close to us and don't let him see you down. We'll ignore them both and enjoy ourselves.," I reply.

"I wonder what category Francis will enter Monique in?" Patricia asks.

"Probably the biggest dog," I answer, and we all laugh again.

The show began at eleven o'clock and Patricia's pies have sold out by noon, so I'm able to pack the table away in the car and spend my time with her and Marjorie. Half an hour later, Marie-Therese and Elise join us and we all sit on the grass to eat lunch. When Arnie lies down he takes up as much room as the rest of us put together. Ollee adores him. He even offers him his chew stick which Arnie polishes off in two bites. We are chatting and laughing and discussing the forthcoming competitions when suddenly a shadow comes over our group as the sun is blocked out by Monique. She is standing in front of us with one hand on her hip and a pouty look on her face.

"Hello, girls," she says. "Are you enjoying yourselves? Lovely event, isn't it?"

Elise looks as if she is about to reply, when Marie-Therese places a staying hand on her arm. Marjorie's face drains of colour.

"I was just saying to Francis, how nice it is to be included in a town event, as a representative of the Mairie."

You could cut the tension with a knife. Suddenly, Patricia springs to her feet. Ollee is startled and begins to bark, and Arnie lifts his large frame from the ground and whines.

"You bitch, you bitch," Patricia screams. "Fuck off, just fuck off, nobody wants you here."

She pushes Monique hard on her shoulder and the young woman stumbles back into a couple walking past. The man steadies her, stopping her from falling. I have rarely heard Patricia swear. She is enraged. I stop her as she goes to step forward again.

"Leave her," I say. "She's not worth it. She's just a stupid girl."

"I want to punch that smug smile off her face," Patricia says. "Let go of me. Let me get at her."

We are all standing now. Both dogs are barking. The couple who stopped have now scurried away. I am gripping Patricia's arm. Marie-Therese is standing between us and Monique.

"Get out of here," Marie-Therese say to Monique. "Get out of here before I arrest you for causing a disturbance."

"But I haven't done anything," Monique protests. "She attacked me."

"That's not how I saw it," Marie-Therese replies.

"Nor me," Elise says. "You kicked things off."

Monique backs away, "I'm going to tell Francis," she threatens.

"That's right, run to daddy," Patricia yells after her.

When she is out of sight Marjorie cries, "Take me home, Danielle. Please take me home. I shouldn't have come here."

I place an arm around her shoulder. "You are not running away, Marjorie. We are all here to support you. You are not the bad one. Stop crying and hold your head up high. If you run away now, you'll never stop running. Show everyone that you're not bothered by them. She's just a silly little whore and your husband is a fool."

She inhales deeply and composes herself. "You're right, Danielle. Of course, you're right. When we finish lunch, I'll visit every stall, and watch every competition. I'll let everybody see me enjoying myself. I won't let that little bitch beat me."

"Good for you," I say. "And we'll be by your side."

Chapter 18

The week progresses quietly with nothing major being reported. Although Marjorie has become like a permanent fixture in our home, as she cannot bear to sit in an empty house and Francis is spending more and more time with Monique. Friday arrives, and I am hopeful of having Saturday off, when two things happen to spoil my plan. Firstly, Marjorie telephones to tell me that Francis is in hospital with a suspected heart attack. I offer to drive her to see him, but she politely refuses, and instead asks me to call in a couple of hours, by which time she'll know more about what's happening.

Then, without prior notice, Valentin Foret arrives in the office.

"I believe you wish to speak to me," he says, offering me a limp, sweaty hand to shake.

Everything about him is unsettling, from his sparse, comb-over hairstyle, to his greasy looking trousers. His skin is shiny and spotty, his mouth is full of broken teeth and his smile is more like a leer. I instantly dislike him. He is creepy and he makes my skin crawl.

"Please, come into my office," I say. "I don't know how much you know about what has happened while you've been on retreat."

He follows me into my room and when we are seated he says, "I know that two of my ex-colleagues are dead. Shame – they were good men. We didn't keep in touch – nothing in common you see. I've chosen a simple life away from the hustle and bustle. Whereas they have gathered valuable assets and accumulated lots of money. They both had bank accounts in Switzerland, I believe."

I'm completely stunned. I had no idea. The truth is, I didn't think to look at their accounts.

"They lived very frugally," I say. "Are you sure about your information?"

"Oh yes, quite sure. The love of money is the root of all evil, and boy, did they love money. Now they're both dead. I suppose evil tracked them down. Probably in the form of one of the little bastards we tried to help." He grins, showing his rotten, brown teeth and I shudder involuntarily. "I own very little," he continues. "Having few possessions is very liberating."

"I'd like to ask you about the records of the home," I say.

He squirms slightly in the chair, stares at me, and gives a slow leer, as if trying to size me up.

"I'm afraid I can't help you there. I think they were destroyed after we closed. Henri would have known, but of course, he's dead. Shame – but nothing I can do. Now if that's all?"

He begins to rise from the chair.

"Please, Monsieur Foret, sit down," I say, and he slowly lowers himself again. "We've located the records. We just need your help in deciphering them."

"How...," he starts, his face stiffens, he's obviously rattled. "Where did you find them?"

"Pere Gregory," I reply. I'm feeling rather smug. Wriggle out of this, I think. Foret has something to hide and I intend to find out what.

I have Marie-Therese bring in the various ledgers from the home and she sits with us as I try to get Foret to explain them. It takes forty minutes for him to tell us what we mostly already know. Namely, the dates of birth of the boys, and when they entered the home. Also listed are the details of their next of kin, where known.

"I'd like to understand what the various codes are, pertaining to the monetary sums," I say.

"I'm afraid I can't help you there," he replies. "I've already told you, I have no interest in money, not now and not then. I survive solely on my pension."

"But you were the record keeper. You must have a basic understanding of these books at the very least," Marie-Therese says. She is frustrated by the man, and so am I.

"Young people always want what they can't have," he says, raising his eyebrows and giving me his creepy leer. "They don't listen, and they have no patience, you see."

He looks pointedly at Marie-Therese. Her face reddens, and I know she's having great difficulty in holding her tongue, but she says nothing. Good girl, I think. He's trying to bait you. Don't rise to it.

"I don't believe you when you say that you had no idea how the home was financed," I say. "Where do you think the money came from to keep you employed?"

"Well now, that's a different question, Officer. I don't understand Henri's scribbling, but I do know that most of the money came from donations. If the boys were contracted out for work experience, the home was paid for their time. We used the placements, and the money derived from them, to further their education."

"And what sort of sums are we talking about here? For the work experience, not the donations?" I ask. "And what kind of work were the boys employed to do?"

He grins again, "I really have no idea," he replies. "As I said before, I don't understand Henri's codes, and they are the key."

"So, you don't know what work they were doing to further their experience and education? How can that be? Were you simply taking a pay packet and not involving yourself with anything to do with the place? Were you blind, Monsieur Foret or did you just not care?"

"I'm finding your questioning rather aggressive, Officer, considering I'm an innocent man simply trying to assist you." He grins again and shakes his finger at me as if I'm a naughty child.

The man is making my blood boil.

"Monsieur, my colleague and I are asking these questions because we are trying to keep you from being murdered. Two people are already dead," I stress.

"That's very considerate of you, officers, but don't waste your time worrying about me. I'll be perfectly safe. I'm returning to Spain later today. I'll be staying with a young friend. No-one will know where I am. And besides, I will not allow myself to be abducted and I have no intention of being driven to suicide. As I said before, I'm an innocent man."

I don't believe for one minute that this obnoxious man is innocent, but neither can I prove he's guilty of anything.

"May I ask you a few more questions about daily life at the home?" Marie-Therese asks.

"Why, my dear? Are you thinking of opening a business? Do you like the idea of running a correctional establishment? I can't think why else your question is relevant to this investigation."

Marie-Therese glances at me. I shake my head, so she doesn't pursue it.

Foret stands and looks at his watch. "Whilst your company is charming, ladies, I must take my leave of you now. I have an appointment. So, unless you are planning to arrest me for something, I'll say au revoir."

He offers me his hand, but I don't take it. I open my office door to allow him to leave. I don't accompany him through the main office and out of the building, but instead I simply shut my door behind him.

"I could kill that man," Marie-Therese says through gritted teeth. "He's ghastly."

"He is horrible," I agree. "Perhaps someone will kill him for you, and if he is murdered, we'll understand why."

After lunch, I receive a call from Marjorie.

"Hello, Danielle," she says. "May I take you up on your kind offer of a lift to the hospital? They've said that Francis has had a small heart attack and they're keeping him in for a few days to do some more tests. I must take him an overnight bag. I don't really care if he has his own things or not, but I don't want the staff talking about me. I'm worried that I'll have difficulty parking close to the ward that he's in. And I'm rather tired. It's all been quite a shock."

"Of course, I'll drive you, no problem," I reply. "I'll just finish off a couple of things here and I'll be with you in about half an hour. Is that okay?"

"Bless you, Danielle. That's perfect."

"Does Monique know about this?" I ask. "Is she likely to be there?"

"He's not allowed any visitors just now, only me, his wife," she replies. "I'm sure Monique would prefer a vibrant, exciting lover, rather than an old has been with a damaged heart, but we'll see. Only time will tell."

"Perhaps, she'll leave him, and you'll be able to return to your normal relationship," I suggest.

"But I don't want him back, Danielle. I want to find a way of divorcing him without losing everything. I've had enough. I want to be rid of him. I want to be rid of Monique as well. I don't want that bitch to win."

Marjorie is waiting at her gate when I arrive. She places a holdall onto the back seat then gets into the passenger seat beside me.

"I'm so glad you're here for me, Danielle. You'll help me to stay strong. I keep crying on and off and I don't seem to be able to stop."

"You've had a bad shock," I reply. "You and Francis have been together for a long time. He's hurt you very badly and now he's ill. You don't know whether to love him or hate him."

"Oh, I hate him. I really hate him. My tears are for all the lost years when we could have had everything – should have had everything. I've wasted the best part of my life loving that man. He's had one affair after another – thinking that if he was discreet, then all was well. All was forgivable. Well I don't forgive him. I can't forgive him."

She dabs at her eyes with a tissue.

"I've missed so much. You know I had little contact with my brother over the years because of Francis' homophobic attitude. And he tried to stop me befriending Patricia when he found out she was a lesbian. He's a narrow-minded bigot and I'm angry with myself for putting up with it for so long. Over the years I've turned myself into a 'Stepford Wife', and for what? To be betrayed with one little whore after another."

We near the hospital. Marjorie sighs deeply and lifts her make-up bag from her handbag.

"I feel better now I've got that off my chest. Thank you for listening. I'm sorry I laid it all on you, but I needed to vent my feelings. I'm ready to face the bastard now, and hopefully, I'll manage it without crying."

When I stop the car, she uses the vanity mirror to touch up her makeup, and I can't help thinking, what a beautiful woman she is. Then she throws a kiss to herself in the mirror before closing it.

"I want him to see what he's losing," she says. "Oh, well, wish me luck."

Marjorie gets out of the car, lifts the holdall from the back seat, and walks towards the hospital entrance. She reaches the door then stops, turns around, and walks quickly back to the car.

"Come with me, Danielle," she begs. "I know you can't come into the room, but please come with me to the ward."

She looks at me pleadingly. "I'm not as brave as I thought I was," she explains.

I jump out of the car and link arms with my friend. "Yes, you are," I reply, reassuringly. "You're the bravest woman I know, and you can do this."

Chapter 19

On Saturday morning our friend Freddy arrives with his friend Alain, the man I met at the party. I'm working in the garden when they step out of Freddy's car.

"Bonjour," I say. "Patricia told me you were visiting. You want a couple of rabbits for the children, I believe."

"Yes, please, Danielle. Two females if you don't mind. I can't put two males together or they'll fight. They're for pets, not for the pot. Patricia said you have lots this year."

"Yes, too many, we can't eat them quickly enough. Would you each like one for the pot as well?"

Alain smiles. "Thanks very much. I only came for the ride and now I'll have tomorrow's dinner too."

"Yes, please Danielle," Freddy says. "Patricia also has a tray of eggs, an apricot tart and eight jars of fig chutney for me. I've brought you twelve bottles of red wine in exchange."

"Sounds like a deal," I reply. "I'll just go and sort out some boxes to hold your rabbits. You can deal with the ones for the pot yourselves, they'll be fresher that way."

Alain's face pales. "What kill them, you mean."

Freddy laughs, "What a weakling you are," he says. "Don't worry, I'll prepare yours for you. I'll even skin it. Then all you'll have to do is cook it."

The men stay with us for an early lunch. As usual, Patricia lays a superb spread which we eat at the table in the garden. We spend the next two hours in the shade of the arbour, devouring the food and chatting.

"Are you still investigating the murders?" Alain asks. "Have you arrested anyone yet?"

"We're still investigating, but we've very little to go on and I fear the case will rapidly grow cold. No arrests yet. We had a potential suspect, but it came to nothing. He was the brother of a boy who committed suicide."

"Christian's older brother? He was a suspect?"

"What do you know about the family?" I ask. "How do you know about Christian?"

"I know he got into trouble at the same time as my cousin Eddy. That's all. They hung out in the same gang."

"When you said one of the boys killed himself, I didn't realise it was someone Eddy knew well. Do you think he might have information that could give us a lead? We can't even work out what work the boys did or how they were educated while they lived at the home. Eddy might help us to make sense of the records. The rest of the people involved have been very tight lipped. Do you think he would talk to me?"

"I'm sure he would. He was always happy to dish the dirt on that place. But you'll have to find him first. He works as a musician now, and he travels around. The last I heard, he was in London."

"Do you have a phone number for him?" I ask.

"I don't, but I can check with my aunt. Unfortunately, they fell out a few months ago, so, it might be a long shot. They're both alike, you see, stubborn and difficult."

"Please do try, Alain. It would be a great help to me if I could speak to him."

"Of course," he replies, "I'll see what I can do."

"Oh, and what's his surname, please? It might assist me if I can find him in the records."

"Martinez. His second name is Martinez."

We exchange telephone numbers before the men rise and prepare to leave.

As they pack the car, Alain asks, "What's the name of my rabbit?"

"Oh, we don't name the rabbits," Patricia replies. "You can't eat them if you name them. As soon as they have a name they become a pet. It would be like eating your child."

Alain gulps and his face drains of colour. He stares at the rabbit in the box. "He looks like an Andre," he says. "Perhaps I'll give him to my daughter, as a pet."

We watch as they drive off. "He'll never eat rabbit again, will he?" Patricia says.

"No, probably not," I reply. "And certainly not Andre."

* * *

Sunday brings a sudden, but thankfully, short lived, storm. I hear the rain battering the window at around six a.m. and it stops me from getting back to sleep. By eight, it's reduced to a drizzle and by nine the sun is out again, and the sky is clear.

The storm makes me think about all the little jobs I must do to ensure our house and garden are ready for the winter months ahead. I begin to construct a mental list. First and foremost, I shall check the roof of the house. As most old houses here are constructed of stone and concrete, there's very little chance of water penetrating. Although, there are one or two areas that depend on the red tiles that cover the roof and that's where I must check that there are no problems.

The rabbit hutches and the hen house will certainly require some attention to make sure they're wind, water and fox proof. We've lost our hens to a fox once before and it's not a pretty sight. The devils are smart and can be desperate enough in winter to take risks.

Cutting back the fire break around the house is another tedious job, but it must be done. And we have a tall, eucalyptus tree that's well and truly dead, and should be removed. The previous owner must have planted the eucalyptus because he liked the look of it, as all the other trees on my property produce something. I can't even use the wood from this tree to burn in the stove as it's full of oil that emits black smoke. I'll put an ad online offering the wood for free to anyone who wants it and can collect it quickly. It might save me several trips to the dump.

I hear Patricia moving around in the kitchen. She'll leave for church soon and I'll begin my chores then. The front door opens with a creak then closes again, another job to be done, I think. The creak will only get worse when the damper weather comes. She must be taking Ollee for a walk. I continue to lie in bed; I'm comfortable and unwilling to move. But when the front door creaks again, heralding their return, I rise. I can't stay here forever.

Patricia and I eat breakfast together. My whole day is planned in my head, then my mobile rings. For some reason my instincts tell me that it's bad news, and I'm not wrong.

A voice I don't recognise says, "Madame, sorry to disturb you on a Sunday morning, but I think you should know that a body has been found at the foot of the devil's bridge. Officers from Ceret are at the scene and are awaiting your arrival or instructions."

A cold chill runs down my spine and I shiver. I thank the caller from the emergency services, hang up and immediately telephone Paul.

"We've got another corpse," I say when he answers.

"Oh, merde," he replies.

"The boys from Ceret are standing guard over the body, but we need to go there. Can you be ready in about twenty minutes and I'll pick you up?"

"I suppose I have no choice," he replies. "I wonder who it is? Maybe it's unconnected to our investigation?"

"I hope you're right, Paul. It's a terrible thing to wish for, but it would suit us better if the corpse is simply a poor tormented soul who took the quickest way out of their pain. The devil's bridge is a favourite jumping off point. Anyway, we'll know soon enough. Get ready, and I'll be with you shortly."

There goes my fully planned day, I think. I now have a reason to avoid starting work on all the tedious jobs, but they'll still be waiting for me tomorrow. A decomposing corpse lying in the warm sun, waits for no man.

Chapter 20

Paul and I are rather subdued as we drive towards Ceret. We are not sure what to expect. We travel in silence until Paul says, "Do you know that the Pont de Diablo was constructed between 1321 and 1341?"

"No, Paul," I reply. "I didn't know that."

"Legend has it that the local people called upon the devil to build it for them and he agreed, providing that he could claim the soul of the first person to cross the bridge. The locals tricked the devil by sending a cat across, and its soul was taken. But for a long time, nobody wanted to cross the bridge, just in case."

"And did the first person to cross, die?" I ask.

"How should I know, I wasn't around then," he says.

Silence resumes.

"The bridge was almost blown up at one point, but it was saved by some official. It was during a conflict, but I don't know which one," Paul says. "Lots of people jump off the bridge to kill themselves. I could tell you a few names and dates if you'd like."

"What is this, Paul!" I exclaim, "a history lesson? Where is all this stuff coming from?"

"I'm just trying to fill the silence," he says. "I'm nervous about what we're going to find when we get to the bridge. I wonder who's dead and what Inspector Gerard will say."

"And you think I'm not nervous?" I reply. "It's my neck on the line where Gerard's concerned, not yours. The buck stops with me. And trust me, a lesson in history and legend will make no difference to the outcome."

"I'm sorry, Boss," he says. "I'll shut up and keep my thoughts to myself."

I feel ashamed. "No, I'm sorry, Paul," I reply. "I know you're just trying to help. We'll be there in five minutes, then we'll know who the corpse is, and we'll know where we stand."

"My money is on Valentin Foret," Paul says. "From what Marie-Therese told me, the smug bastard had it coming. She was spitting bullets after your meeting with him. She said he's a truly obnoxious creep."

"Perhaps, but it could also be Luke Mayer. He's a tortured soul and might wish to end it all with a grand gesture."

We arrive, and I park my car at the entrance to the bridge, beside a fire truck.

"Well, Paul, this is it," I say.

I'm aware of both of us inhaling deeply as we climb out of the car.

"Into the valley of death...," Paul mutters, and I know just how he feels.

Doctor Picard is waiting for us. He is the polar opposite of my friend, Poullet, tall and rail thin, his clothes are immaculate. He has one of the best handlebar moustaches in the entire region. Indeed, he has won competitions with his moustache. His shoes are so highly polished, you can see your face in them, and he is polite, he never swears. I can't fault the man, but I miss my friend Poullet. I wish the old devil was here.

"Bonjour, Doctor," I say. "Have you viewed the body yet?"

"No, officer, not yet. Like you, I have just arrived. The pompiers have been down to the bottom of the drop, where the body lies. They have advised that we put on protective clothing as there's a lot of blood and brain matter. The fire chief, standing over there, said his head hit a rock and cracked like a watermelon."

Too much information for a Sunday morning, I think, and my stomach churns.

"Look boys, here she is, the kiss of death," a voice says, purposely loud so I can hear.

It's Jean, my old friend. He's the fire chief on this call and I'm so pleased to see him. At least one of my friends is here to support me.

"Jean, how are you? What have we got?"

"I don't know who he is. There is no I.D. on the guy, but he looks old. There is a puddle of vomit on the bridge above where he went over. It smells of alcohol and there are two partially digested tablets in the vomit. The forensic boys will arrive sometime, but I'm not sure when. They've been informed about the body by the cops from Ceret. However, it is Sunday and they're coming from Perpignan, so it could take a while. Oh, and one other thing, the corpse is naked."

"Oh, mon Dieu, naked, you say? Have you found his clothes?"

"No, not a single item."

"So, it's not suicide?"

"Not unless it's assisted, or he walked from somewhere bare as the day he was born. Which is possible I suppose. He probably went over the bridge in the middle of the night, so perhaps nobody was around to see him."

"We'd better go and have a look at him," I suggest. "Is it possible for us to climb down? We'll need the doctor there too."

"There's a track we can follow," Jean says. "It's not too steep and my men will be on hand to assist you. But suit up first, it's messy down there, and his feet have landed beyond the water's edge."

The doctor purses his lips in distaste. "Can someone lend me boots?" he asks. "These shoes are my Sunday best. My wife polished them this morning for me. She'll be most upset if they're damaged."

"No problem, doc, I'm sure we'll find something to fit you in the truck," Jean replies.

The doctor nods his head then swallows hard. I can see he's nervous. It's normally Poullet who attends the very small number of unusual deaths that we must to deal with here. But of course, in this case, he can't. I think of Poullet and smile. He'll miss the extra money, I think. He hates to let the opportunity of extra cash pass him by.

Paul and I strip down to our underwear and struggle into our protective suits. Doctor Picard glances at us and then pointedly looks away. He is still holding his suit and hasn't yet attempted to put it on.

"Is that really necessary?" he asks, a look of distaste on his face. "I think I'll wear this thing over my clothes," he adds, clutching his protective suit.

"You might manage to get into it because you're really thin," Paul replies. "But your clothes will become sweat soaked rags in minutes in this heat. Soggy underpants are bad enough, but trousers and shirt as well, ugh!"

"I see, I see," Picard replies, and he looks around for somewhere discreet to get changed.

"Oh, for goodness sake, go behind the fire truck," Paul says. He's exasperated with the man. "It's not as if we haven't seen it all before, and you're a doctor," he adds.

"Well you haven't seen me before," Picard protests. "And neither of you are my patients."

He marches off behind the fire truck. Ten minutes pass and he hasn't returned.

"Where is the old duffer?" Paul says. "How long does it take to strip off?"

At that point, Picard walks towards us with his clothes in a neatly folded bundle.

"Do you think he was a valet in a previous life?" Paul mutters.

"I'll just put my belongings in my car," the doctor says, and he heads off across the bridge.

"Where on earth is he going," Paul splutters.

"He's parked on the other side," Jean explains.

"Oh, mon Dieu, I never thought I'd say this, but give me Poullet any day."

"I'll tell him you said that, Paul," I say. "He'll be delighted."

"Don't you dare," he replies.

We finally begin our descent. It's not easy as it's rather steep. From time to time, loose stones roll away beneath our feet causing us to slide. Doctor Picard insists on one of the firemen holding his arm to steady him, and it's probably just as well. His limbs seem to stick out in all directions like a discarded doll and his coordination is all over the place.

"It won't be Luke Mayer if it's an older man," Pauls says. "My money's still on Foret."

"You're probably right," I reply.

I'm already trying to plan what I'll say to Inspector Gerard. He'll want to know why we didn't protect the only surviving man from the team who ran the home. Even although Valentin refused our help, we should have tried a bit harder. At least Marie-Therese will be able to back up my story.

We reach the bottom of the track and walk only about ten metres to the body. Paul is breathing deeply, he's rather squeamish at the best of times and this is a mess.

"Stand back, Paul," I offer. "Only one of us has to do this."

He doesn't wait, but back steps to the foot of the track.

The way the man has fallen, his head has hit a sharp rock and is almost split in two. His face is covered in blood. His arms and legs are twisted with bits of bone sticking through the flesh, and his back is bent oddly, as if it's been broken.

"Do I need to go any closer?" the doctor asks. "I can declare him dead from here."

"No, Doc, it's okay. Your work is over for the day. You can go home," I say.

"Thank you," he replies. "And, if you don't mind, I prefer Doctor Picard, not Doc," he adds. "It's more professional."

"What a pompous ass," Jean says. "Why isn't Poullet here? Why were we stuck with that old fart?"

I explain about Poullet's connection and Jean is sympathetic.

"So, do you know who the corpse is?" Jean asks.

"Probably Valentin Foret, but it's hard to tell with all the blood on the face and the body naked. Would you mind wiping the face, so I can see it better, then I might recognise him."

Jean throws some river water over the face then washes it with a rag, and immediately, I realise who it is.

"Oh, merde," I say. it's not Valentin after all.

"Paul, get over here," I call. "I need you to see this and confirm it. I think the corpse is Pere Gregory."

Chapter 21

Once I get over my initial shock, my thoughts turn to the investigation. Somehow, I must protect myself from criticism. I need a suspect or at the very least a lead before this murder hits the headlines.

I go and speak to Jean. "Who found the body? Is the person around?" I ask.

"The man who found the corpse is a rough sleeper. He's a drunk. His hovel is over there."

Jean points in the direction of the bridge.

"There's a natural dip in the land and he's constructed a kind of tent with branches and plastic sheeting. I don't know how many days he's been camping there, but there are empty wine bottles all around it."

"Did he hear Pere Gregory fall?"

"No, he was dead to the world from drink. He wouldn't have heard a thing, even if it blew up in his face. He got up in the morning, went to have a piss in the river, and practically fell over the body."

"Where is he now? Has he run off?"

"No, when he found the corpse he got such a shock that he fainted and hit his head when he fell. He knocked himself out. When he came round, he managed to call for the emergency services. By the time we arrived he was only semi-conscious. We weren't sure if his state was caused by the alcohol he'd consumed or by him hitting his head when he blacked out. Anyway, we sent him to hospital in Perpignan just in case."

"It always amazes me that so many rough-sleeping drunks, with little means of support, can still afford a mobile phone," I say.

"I see it all the time," Jean replies. "I can barely afford my bills and I'm working every day. Sometimes one of the charities gives them a phone. I suppose it's a lifeline for them. Their hardly likely to use much credit, living on the edge of society as they do. Who are they going to call?"

I thank Jean for the information then say goodbye to him. Then Paul and I return to my car.

"What the hell do we do now?" he asks.

I think for a moment.

"Get on your phone, Paul," I instruct. "I want Cedric or Bernard to find someone to accompany them, pick up Valentin Foret and take him to the office. I don't care if they're not on call – I want one of them to get him. They can use any means. Charge him with obstruction if they must, but I want him brought in, before he has a chance to leave for Spain. As he's the only one still alive out of the group, he is now our main suspect. Get one of the other cops, who works out of our office, to investigate the bank accounts of all of the men. Foret said something about Henri and Roland having large amounts of money. I want to know how much and where it is. I want this investigation to be kept in house, so only our people are to be kept in the loop. As it's Sunday, they may find nobody to help them until tomorrow, but banks often have twenty-four-hour emergency numbers, so you never know. While you do that, I am going to telephone Junot and give him a story. I want us to control what's reported."

"Okay, Boss, I'm on it," Paul replies.

I feel invigorated because I have a plan of action. Many people might think I'm rather lazy, because much of my job involves public relations, with my officers doing the grunge work. The truth is, I don't put myself out if I can help it. Why should I? But when something as serious as murder occurs, I must to be seen to be proactive. I climb out of the car, lean against the door, and dial Junot's number. He answers almost immediately.

"Bonjour, Danielle," he says. "Have you got something for me?"

"And bonjour to you too," I reply. "Do you sit with your phone in your hand waiting for me to call?" I ask.

"Pretty much," he replies. "I have a sad life."

I laugh. "Well, today's your lucky day, Junot," I say. "I'm going to give you your scoop, but you must use it right away. It won't be long until it's the talk of the town."

Junot is standing outside the office when we return. He is fidgety with excitement.

"I won't forget that you're giving me this opportunity," he says. "There will come a time when you'll want a story published and I'll be your man. You've heard of the power of the press – well I have that power."

"Come on Superman," Paul says, smiling. "Let's go inside. We could all do with a coffee."

We go straight through to my office and Paul switches on the coffee maker. "We've no fresh milk so it will have to be black," he states.

"I brought this with me," Junot says, taking a Dictaphone from his pocket. "Do you mind if I use it?"

"Does that thing really work? It looks like an antique," Paul says.

"I have no objection," I state. Then I begin, "Pere Gregory was found dead this morning in suspicious circumstances."

Junot draws in his breath. "In what way, suspicious?" he asks. "I take it he's been murdered."

"He was stark naked," I reply.

Junot grins with delight, "Can I have a photograph? This will sell millions of newspapers."

I ignore him then continue to tell him what I want him to hear.

"So, nobody else has this story. How long do I have before your press officer gets it?" he asks.

"The story could break at any time. After we finish here, I'm going to tell Pere Gregory's housekeeper that her employer is dead. The pompiers and the Ceret cops have been asked not to speak about it, but who knows? Everyone loves a bit of gossip. However, I am about to give you your scoop. You'll be the only reporter who knows we have a suspect and we're holding him for questioning."

"Really, so you know who the killer is?" Junot rubs his hands together. His eyes dart from me to Paul.

I hear voices in the outer office. Paul stands and opens the door. "Bernard and Marie-Therese are here," he states, "And they have him."

"We'll be finished in here shortly," he calls to them. "Thanks for coming in. So much for having Sunday off, eh?" he adds.

Junot jumps to his feet. "Who is here? Is it the man? Is the suspect out there? Can I speak to him?"

I reply in the order the questions were delivered. "Valentin Foret. Yes. Yes. And no, certainly not. Sit down Junot. You'll have everything you need to know."

"Why is Foret a suspect?" he asks.

"He's the only person closely connected to the running of the home who's still alive. He has information about the encoded records of the home, but he's refusing to help us. He mentioned that large sums of money were involved, but says he received none of it, and that all the money went to Henri Boudin and Roland Michel. Perhaps he did get money and it's well hidden. He told us the other two had Swiss bank accounts, but we've yet to confirm that. Other sources have said the boys who resided at the home were hired out as slave labour. However, this too must be confirmed. At this precise time, everything is hearsay and conjecture, so ensure you break the story carefully. You can, however, state categorically that you saw Valentin Foret brought in for questioning and held in custody for refusing to help the police with their enquiries."

"Wow," he says. "This is magic."

"I thought it would make your day," I reply.

He switches off his Dictaphone. "Off the record, do you think Foret's the killer?" Junot asks.

"Maybe, maybe not. At this stage it's too early to tell. But he'll do for now. Now if you don't mind, Junot, I must ask you to leave. I have a suspect to interview."

"Of course, no problem. I'm leaving right now. I've got a scoop to write. Do you want me to run it past you before I sell the story? I'm planning to send it to the national which took my last piece."

"Not necessary, I trust you," I say. "Besides it's your neck on the line not mine, if you go to print with something libellous."

I show Junot out of my room and walk him through the main office to the front door. He peers at Foret as he passes him.

"He doesn't look much like a killer," Junot says. "He's an old man."

"He's in his sixties," I reply. "To you he's an old man, but to an eighty-year-old, he's a boy. And what age do you think a serial killer should be? The English doctor, Harold Shipman, was in his mid-fifties when he was arrested."

"I suppose I hadn't really thought about it," Junot replies. "It's just that Foret looks so ordinary."

"Most psychopaths do," I reply. "For all you know I might be a psychopath, or Paul could be one, or even your grandmother. That's why they're so difficult to catch. And when a psychopath is also a sociopath, then the bodies can begin to pile up."

"So, is Foret is psychopath or a sociopath?"

"Perhaps neither, perhaps both. Might I suggest you include a factual definition in your article, without attributing either description to Monsieur Foret. That way you can plant the seed in your readers minds without stepping over the line. They'll draw their own conclusions, I'm sure."

"Brilliant, Danielle! That's a great idea. It will boost the story. Everyone loves a psycho!"

"Everyone except their victims, I suspect," I reply.

I watch him run down the road. He can't wait to write my story. This will be such a scoop for him, and the public will love me.

When I get back to my room, Paul has moved Foret there, and they are both seated at my desk.

"Am I under arrest, Officer?" Foret asks. "Because I must warn you, I'm not happy to be here again. I have nothing more to say to you."

I stare at him, long and hard. He tries to meet my eyes, but he cannot and after a few moments he turns away. This tells me a lot. This tells me he has something to hide.

"Coffee?" I offer.

"I don't intend to be here long enough to drink it," he replies, giving his creepy smile.

"Suit yourself," I say. "Would you like a coffee, Paul?" I ask. "This may take a while."

"Thank you, Boss," he says, and he winks at me. He understands the need for me to take charge and to have the upper hand.

"Now Monsieur Foret, let us begin," I say. "I want you to be perfectly clear; we are not leaving this room until I have a better understanding of what went on at the home. I want to know what it was like for the boys on a day to day basis."

"And precisely what has any of that to do with the murders?"

"I'm not sure, but I feel that the treatment of the residents might hold the key to opening up the cases."

"And if I choose not to comment? Will you really carry out your threat and arrest me? A good lawyer could have me released in under an hour. You have no grounds to charge me."

That's when I formally charge him with obstruction.

"You'd better contact your lawyer, Monsieur Foret," I say.

Paul stares at me. His look is one of pure admiration. "I'll fetch a charge sheet, Boss. Start emptying your pockets, Foret," he says. Paul stands.

"Wait, wait," Foret replies. He's holding his hands up as if in defence. "There's no need for this. If I tell you about the money, can I go?"

"Start talking and we'll see," I reply.

He begins, "Every penny of the charitable donations was ploughed back into the home. The boys were well fed; they had clean, serviceable uniforms to wear; the home was kept cool in summer and warm in winter. In short, it was run to a very high standard. We were regularly inspected by the board of directors, including your mayor, and they were satisfied with what they saw. If you bring me the records, I'll explain the accounting."

Paul leaves the room to fetch the books. When he leaves Foret leans across the table.

"Don't push me too far, Officer," he hisses at me, I feel his spittle hit my face. "I'm in close contact with the mayor. He owes me a couple of favours. He can destroy you," he warns.

I'm shocked, he's threatening me, and he waited for Paul to leave the room so there were no witnesses. The door opens. He sits back in his chair. Paul enters the room carrying a ledger. I'm unsure of myself, so I say nothing about his threat. Instead, I hand Foret the ledger. He flicks through the pages before stopping at one with a column of numbers, then turns the book to face me.

"This is the first year of us being in business," he says. "Every page after this one is similar and represents the following years. The entries in this column are the charitable donations. As you can see, they are fully documented with a code. The codes refer to the person or company who donated the money."

"And, how can we decipher who those people or businesses were. Do you have the corresponding names and addresses?"

"No, I don't. If they still exist, the priest would have had them."

"And what about these figures?" I ask, pointing to a second column with much larger amounts.

He stares at me for a minute as if contemplating what to say. A slow, ghastly smile crosses his lips.

"These are the numbers you really want to understand, Officer. These represent the money earned by the boys for their sterling efforts. This is where Henri and Roland built their fortunes."

I flick through the following pages, taking account of all the years, and do a quick calculation. It runs to over three million euros.

"Oh, mon Dieu," I say. "It's a fortune. And the boys, the residents, made all this money for you and your colleagues. You hired them out as slave labour."

"Be careful what you say, Officer. You wouldn't want to be charged with slander. It wasn't forced labour. It was education. The boys had the opportunity to learn a trade. It just so happened that the home was paid for their efforts."

"By the home, you mean Henri, Roland and yourself."

"As I said before, Henri and Roland amassed large sums which they put into bank accounts overseas. If their accounts are in Switzerland as I suspect, you'll never find the money. No self-respecting Swiss banker would ever release their client's details."

"How is it that they had cash, but you don't?" I ask.

"As I told you before, I live a simple life. I have a small apartment here, but I spend most of my time on retreat in Spain, in the mountains. It's very peaceful in the mountains away from the hustle and bustle of everyday life. It's idyllic."

"Where exactly in Spain do you spend this idyllic time?" I ask.

A nervous look passes over his face. He licks his lips. "It's a small place, just outside Camprodon, only the retreat and a handful of houses are there. It's just a hamlet really."

"And the name of the retreat?" I press.

He swallows hard. "El Castillo," he replies.

I turn to my computer and Google the name, and there it is, El Castillo. It is used as a retreat, but not by hippy types as Foret led me to believe. It's a five-star, spa resort, frequented by the rich and famous. I check further – there's a photo of Valentin Foret, wearing white linen, with his arm around the shoulders of a much younger man. They are both grinning. The item introduces Foret as the owner. Now I know why he has no money to show. It's all been ploughed into building the retreat.

I swivel the computer round so he can see the screen.

"Rather impressive," I say. "Who is the young man?"

"My partner, Eric," he replies. "We've been together for several years."

"And was he a former resident of the home?"

"We fell in love when he was living there, if that's what you want to know. He was over the age of consent. We did nothing wrong."

Paul is outraged. "You molested the boys you were meant to protect."

"I molested no-one," he says, standing up and raising his voice. "They came to me. They loved me. I protected them from Pere Gregory; he was very strict with them."

"Please sit down," I say, and he slumps back into the chair.

Paul swipes a tear from his eye, takes a handkerchief from his pocket and blows his nose.

"Oh, mon Dieu," he says. "You bastards tortured these boys. Their lives must have been a living hell."

"No, I told you, they were well fed and clothed. They were cared for."

"They did all the work," Paul protests. "That's why you only had one house-keeper. You didn't care for them, these boys looked after you."

"They learned discipline. We saved the police a lot of work. Few of them reoffended."

"You really believe that you did no harm, don't you?" I say. "You truly think you were simply innocent benefactors?"

"Of course, we were innocent. We helped the boys and the community."

"And you helped yourselves along the way," Paul says.

"Maybe so," he concedes.

"You were all criminals," Paul adds. "Cruel child abusers."

Foret inhales. "I think not," he says. "But if you believe that, then you must prove it."

We sit in silence while I gather my thoughts. My mind is racing. I must go and inform Pere Gregory's housekeeper of his death and I also want to search his house to see if there are any further records. I want those names and addresses. I don't want Foret to have the opportunity of calling someone and perhaps get access to them before me.

"Please excuse me for a moment," I say, and I go to the outer office where Bernard and Marie-Therese are waiting.

"Paul and I must go out," I say. "I want you to keep Foret here until we return. Offer him food, but don't let him leave, whatever he threatens. We'll be as quick as we can. He might ask for his lawyer and that's fine. It's Sunday, so he'll have a hard time getting anyone. If he refuses to stay, as a last resort, charge him with obstruction. But only as a last resort. He's a nasty piece of work. Don't be intimidated by him. Okay?"

"Fine, Boss," Bernard says.

Marie-Therese looks more uncertain, but she nods her agreement.

I return to my room. "Would you come with me for a moment, Paul?" I ask. "Please excuse us Monsieur Foret, someone will be with you shortly."

We leave the room, and I explain to Paul what's happening.

As we head for my car Paul says, "He's going to go ballistic when he realises we've gone.

"Good," I reply. "That bastard deserves to be upset."

Chapter 22

It doesn't take long for us to reach the street where Pere Gregory's house is situated, and as we turn into it, I can see the priest's car parked at the end, a distance from his front gate. When Paul and I investigate we find the car unlocked and the keys in the ignition. His clothes and personal belongings are on the front seat. I immediately call Perpignan to request forensics to attend.

"Someone brought this car back and parked it here. Just out of sight of the house," Paul says.

"Whoever it was, he's our killer," I reply. "The housekeeper must have expected Pere Gregory to be away overnight as he's wasn't reported missing. If she left the house to go to church this morning, she wouldn't have walked past the car parked at this end of the street. And besides, she wouldn't have been looking for it."

We make our way to the house and ring the doorbell. There's a shuffling sound, and the turning of a key then Madame Ohms opens the door.

"Pere Gregory is not here," she says when she sees us. "He's visiting his friend who lives in Spain and he won't be back until tomorrow."

"May we come in, please," I say. "I have some news for you."

For a moment she eyes me suspiciously then she leads us down the narrow hallway to the parlour. She indicates for us to sit. "Would you like some coffee?" she offers.

"Paul can fetch us coffee. Sit down with me please, Madame Ohms," I say.

A look of panic crosses her face. "What's happened?" she asks. "Something's wrong, isn't it? Has Pere Gregory been hurt? Has there been an accident?"

I usher her to a chair. "I'm very sorry to inform you, Madame, but Pere Gregory is dead."

She slumps forward, and I hold her bony shoulders to steady her. "Go and get that coffee, Paul. Plenty of sugar. She's had a bad shock," I say.

"Cognac. There's cognac in the decanter on the side table. Please pour me a small glass," she asks.

I do as she requests, and she sips it. Gradually her colour returns.

Paul brings a pot of coffee and three small cups. We sit at the table and drink it down before any of us speaks again.

"How did he die?" she asks. "Did he crash his car? I kept telling him to have his eyes tested. I'm sure he needed new glasses."

"No, Madame, it was nothing like that. I'm afraid he's been murdered."

"Oh, mon Dieu, why? Why would anyone want to harm him?"

"That's what we're trying to find out," I reply. "Who was Pere Gregory going to meet? You said it was his friend from Spain."

"Valentin Foret. They used to work together. Two of their old work colleagues died recently and they wanted to talk about it."

She pauses and contemplates what she's said. "They too were murdered, weren't they? You must warn Monsieur Foret. He may be in grave danger." She begins to cry.

"Don't upset yourself, Madame," I say, and I take her hand in mine and gently rub the back of it. "We have Monsieur Foret at the police station. He's in safe hands."

Paul pours more coffee and we sip the rich, dark liquid.

"We'd like to have a look about the house, if you have no objection. Perhaps we'll find some clues that will give us some leads."

"Of course, Officer. Go ahead, do whatever you have to," she replies.

I nod to Paul and he begins the search. I stay seated with Madame Ohms to distract her from the intrusion.

"I don't know what I'll do," she says. "This is Pere Gregory's house. Where will I go now that he's dead? What will become of me? Where will I live?" Her shoulders shake, and great sobs escape from her lips.

I place my arm around her. She's so skinny and fragile, it's like holding a little sparrow.

"Don't think about it just now, Madame," I say. "You have no need to worry, the church will look after you. You might find that you'll be able to continue living here."

My words help to reassure her, and after a while she stops weeping and dries her eyes. We talk about Pere Gregory and her life in this house for another twenty minutes before Paul returns to the room. He looks triumphant. In his hands he's holding a ledger and a laptop computer.

"Have you someone we can contact to stay with you?" I ask Madame Ohms.

"My friend Audrey lives next door," she replies. "Would you mind going round and knocking on her door to see if she's home?"

Paul disappears out of the room and returns a few minutes later with the neighbour.

"We can go now, Boss," he says to me. "Audrey will look after Madame Ohms."

We take our leave, and I'm pleased to be out of the house. So, I think, Pere Gregory was going to meet Foret, funny he didn't tell us anything about that.

"Back to the office?" Paul asks.

"Oh, yes," I reply. "And we are going to charge Valentin Foret with obstruction. It will allow us to keep him in France for the next day or two at least, and stop him from running off over the border to Spain. Either he's the murderer or he's likely to be the next victim. One way or the other, we need to know where he is."

By the time we get back to the office it's after six. I telephone Patricia to let her know that I might be very late, so she won't worry.

"Don't forget to eat something," she says, and I assure her I'll be okay.

I have Bernard run to the baker for some cold savoury snacks and whatever cakes they have left, then I let him go home. Paul and I will continue to interview Valentin Foret. There is much for him to explain and I don't care if it takes us all night to extract the information. He will give me the answers I need.

Paul puts the food onto plates and we take it to my room where Foret is seated.

"Ah, dinner is served," he says, as the food is placed on the desk. "Is this the best you could do? Well, I suppose it's Sunday evening now. We should all be going home for our evening meal, not feasting on the dried-out remnants of the baker's shop."

"Valentin Foret," I say. "You are being formally charged with obstruction." I read him his rights. A look of fear flashes in his eyes. Not so smug now, I think.

"This is ridiculous!" he exclaims. "I've been helping you. I'm still here waiting to help you. How are my actions causing obstruction?"

He is outraged, and he stands up and looks around the room like a trapped animal. Good, I think, I've finally got him on the back foot.

"Sit down, Foret," Paul says, and I note the subtle change. He's dropped saying 'Monsieur' before his name.

Foret does as he is told. I open the ledger in front of him.

"I want you to decipher the codes in this book, and explain how they correspond to the other ledger," I say. "I want to know which companies benefited from the work carried out by your residents."

"If I explain everything will you drop the charge?" he asks.

"At this time, I'm not prepared to discuss anything but the information I've asked for," I reply. "Let's get on with it. I don't want to be here all night."

It takes him no more than twenty minutes. The scenario was simple. Dupont, the builder was also a board member; he hired the boys to work for his company then he paid the home. The mayor before Francis and subsequently Francis himself, gave all the major town work to Dupont, innocently thinking they were merely helping a colleague. Matthew Bryce, the third member of the board, signed off the work and asked no questions. For his compliance, he received teaching work at the home, for which he was generously paid. Dupont could pick up the best jobs in the area because he could undercut everyone else on price. It was a perfect set-up.

"So, let me get this straight," I say. "Everybody involved, except for the two mayors, who were board members over a long period of time, made money. The mayors unwittingly supplied the bulk of the paying work, but received no personal gain."

"They felt good about helping the home, and their gardens were always immaculate. So, they gained something from their assistance," Foret replies, grinning. "Isn't it funny that many people in high office, the so-called smart ones, can be very trusting and gullible?"

"Hilarious," Paul replies. "I bet you laughed all the way to the bank."

"We all did," Foret says, smugly.

I know Francis will be horrified when he realises how he's been duped. His reputation could be ruined, and while he's with Marjorie, she could be ruined too. Perhaps being divorced from him might be the best thing for her. It could save her reputation, as people would be sympathetic towards her.

"I'm going to release you now," I say to Foret. "But you must stay in the area. I may need to question you further. I want you to hand your passport into the office tomorrow. It will be returned to you if the charge against you is dropped."

"When the charge against me is dropped you mean," he replies. "I'll be back tomorrow with my legal representative."

"As you wish," I reply, and I show him out of the door.

"This case is a can of worms," Paul says. "Where do we go from here?"

"I'm not sure, Paul. I'm too tired to think. Let's just go home. Tomorrow is another day," I reply.

Chapter 23

On Monday I don't get into the office until late morning. I told Paul not to come in until the afternoon as we were both very tired after our marathon day yesterday.

After gathering my thoughts, I telephone Inspector Gerard to give him an update. I tell him most of the information I have, and apart from asking me to make a brief statement to the press officer, he seems satisfied to let me carry on with the investigation.

"I find the manner of the deaths unusual," he says. "Hanging, wrist slashing then a naked jumper. Do you think the murderer is trying to tell us something? Somewhere in his past, something must have made him very angry. He needs his victims to know why they're going to die. You might want to look into this, Danielle. I think the methods of the deaths are significant."

"I'll do that, sir," I say. "Thank you, sir."

We end the call.

"And fuck off, sir," I add when he's gone. Does he think I'm a fool? Of course, the murderer is leaving a message. Otherwise why not just shoot his victims. That's when I know for sure that Foret is not the killer. He's a manipulator who doesn't like to get his hands dirty. If he wanted the others dead, he would simply have paid a professional to take them out. He can afford it. And he certainly wouldn't bother with the circus show. It's too high risk. Although I can't stand the bastard, and part of me would be glad to see him gone, I must try to protect him, as he's the obvious choice for the next victim.

Just after lunch Foret arrives in the office. He is accompanied by one of the best known avocats in the region, Guy Dechamps. I show them through to my office and, as Paul has yet to appear, I ask Marie-Therese to join us.

"I am here to represent Monsieur Foret," Dechamps says. "I would prefer it if we can keep this meeting as informal and as brief as possible."

"I too," I reply. "As you know, your client has been charged with obstructing the law. We were forced to charge him, even though he was given the opportunity, on more than one occasion, to avoid such action. I assume you are familiar with the case?"

"Yes, I have been fully advised by my client."

"Three men are now dead. All were colleagues of your client. We believe that Monsieur Foret is in grave danger of being the fourth victim, and we are trying to protect him."

"Absolute rubbish!" Foret exclaims. "This officer is a homophobic bigot. She hates that I live with a younger man. If I hang around here, she'll probably lead the murderer to my door. You know what I'm like, Guy," he says, addressing the avocat. "You lived at the home for two years when your parents couldn't cope. Now look at you. You're one of the most successful and respected men in Perpignan. So, I must have done something right."

We are all stunned by his outburst. Dechamps' face is red as a beetroot. I'm seething. Marie-Therese is open mouthed. It takes me a moment to find my voice.

"I am not homophobic, and I am not a bigot," I begin. "My sister, who I live with and adore, is a lesbian. I have no problem with your lifestyle. It's true that I dislike you, Monsieur Foret, but that doesn't stop me from doing my job. If you disappear from this town, we won't be able to protect you, neither will we know if something happens to you. By not explaining the codes in the ledgers, you put everyone connected to the home at risk. Perhaps if you had been more forthcoming, Pere Gregory might still be alive."

Dechamps squirms in his seat. He is obviously uncomfortable and embarrassed. I'm sure he would rather we did not know of his past.

"I must apologise for my client," he says. "He's under tremendous pressure. I'm sure he didn't mean to offend you, Officer."

"Oh, but he did," I reply.

Foret has the good grace to stare at his feet. He knows he's gone too far.

"Why don't we bring this meeting to a close?" Dechamps suggests. "My client will give you his passport and he will not leave town. Once I have had a chance to discuss his situation with him, we'll make an appointment to return here.

I'm sure he'll want to help you in any way he can with the ledgers, but for the time being, we need to consider our position."

As I can't force any further information out of Foret, I agree with Dechamps' proposal. We all stand, and I'm about to show them out when Dechamps says, "Oh, and one other thing, I take it that you'll be appointing officers to protect my client?"

"No," Foret says, raising his voice. "Absolutely not. I refuse police protection."

"But Valentin," Dechamps replies, "you heard the officer. She just wants to help you."

"She can keep her help," Foret spits. "I don't trust her."

He storms out of the office. Dechamps looks embarrassed. "I'm sorry, very sorry," he says, before hurrying after his client.

I return to my room and shut the door, discouraging any intrusion. Then I place my elbows on the desk and hold my head in my hands. I hated having to defend myself and how I live. The fact that I reside with my friend who's a lesbian is nobody's business but mine. I'm pleased Foret refused my help because I can't stand the man. I don't care if he lives or dies. My only interest in his wellbeing is to stop me from looking bad.

Picking up the phone, I call Patricia. I need to hear a friendly voice.

"Hello, darling," I say, when she answers.

"You sound tired," she says. "Are you okay?"

"Much better for speaking to you. It's been a difficult day."

"I'm glad you called. Marjorie's just left here. Francis has been released from hospital. His heart attack was minor. They think he has angina. He told Marjorie he wants to speak to you. Something about his connection to the boys' home."

"Well he'll have to wait, I'm afraid," I reply. "I'm far too busy today. In fact, I'd better go and get on with work or I'll never get out of here. I just wanted to hear your voice. See you later, darling."

"Love you," she replies. "Don't work too hard. A bientot." I hear a click and she's gone.

In his post as mayor, Francis has the right to know if any member of the community is at risk, because he represents the town and everyone in it. But I don't wish to speak to him. My position should never be compromised, and he's already tried to warn me off regarding Monique. Every municipal worker is frightened to criticise his behaviour because he can affect their jobs, but I can't let him bully me. I'm just not sure how to handle the situation. I need to clear my head, so I leave the office and take a walk by the riverside.

Everything is as usual. Groups of people are playing petanque, dogs are being walked and to my great delight, Byron is sitting on a bench, reading a magazine. He stands as I approach and greets me with a kiss.

"Antiques," he says. "The magazine, not me," he explains, showing me his publication. "Although I'm not far off being one myself," he adds, laughing. "What brings you here?"

"Dilemmas – far too many dilemmas," I reply. "I'm under a lot of pressure, so I had to get out of the office for some air."

"Sit down, dear girl. Tell your uncle Byron all about it. A problem shared is a problem halved and all that rubbish." He smiles kindly and I already feel more relaxed. "But seriously, do you want to talk?" he asks.

Over the next hour, I find myself blurting out everything that's troubling me, and I must admit I feel much better for it.

"I wish that girl would move on from Francis. It must be hell for Marjorie," Byron says. "What on earth does Monique see in him? He's old enough to be her father."

"Money and position," I reply. "It's a powerful drug."

"If you ask me," he says, "she's at the root of your problems. Francis will do anything to defend her, even if it means hurting his friends and family, or in the case of these murders, putting himself at risk. If you could get rid of her, everything would settle down. Then he'd probably go back to being the useless ass he's always been."

"Easier said than done," I reply.

But I have listened to Byron and taken on board all he's said. Consequently, I've decided that Monique and I must have a little chat. Perhaps I can scare her off, or at the very least, persuade her to tone down her behaviour in public. It's embarrassing for people to have to watch her clinging on to Francis and kissing him passionately in full view of the town. Like it or not, they are both public officials, and that sort of behaviour is simply unacceptable. I can only imagine how poor Marjorie must feel.

Chapter 24

I wake the next morning at seven, with Ollee's wet nose in my ear. When I open my eyes, he licks my face excitedly and whimpers. He wants out and I know Patricia's bedroom door must be shut because she would have been his first choice of a companion.

"Okay, Ollee, okay. Go down boy. - Off the bed. - Let me get up."

Once I am dressed, he's very insistent, so, no time for coffee. I haven't even had a shower yet. But the crisp early morning air is pleasant, even if it is still dark and, as I walk, I think about the day ahead. We are already on our way back when I remember that today is meant to be my day off and I could have had a lie in.

I am nervous and anxious most of the time these days because of the huge work load I'm having to cope with. So, whilst I'll telephone the office through-out the day, I'll try to avoid physically going into work – I need the break. I still haven't returned Francis' call because I'm not sure what to say to him. I can guess what he wants to say to me and I know I won't like it. However, there are two calls I must make today; one to Doctor Poullet, who's been surprisingly restrained, but needs to be given an update, and the other to Freddy to tell him we've been enjoying his wine and want to buy a further two cases to give as gifts at Christmas. Other than that, I have no plans.

Patricia and I have breakfast together. She's going to meet my papa at the orchard and help him to finish preparing it for the winter months ahead. He began the work a while ago and today should see the job complete. I've made repairs to the henhouse and the rabbit hutches. Fortunately, there wasn't much work to be done with them. I like this time of year, when everything is winding down for winter, yet there's a flurry of excitement about the holidays to come.

"I've invited your mama and papa for Christmas lunch," Patricia says. "Oh, and Byron too. He'll drive your mama and papa, so you won't have to."

"It's only just become November and already you're planning Christmas lunch," I reply. "Will you be organising Easter in December?"

"Probably," she says, smiling. "You know I like to be organised. Speaking about being that, can you drive me to the market in Ceret next weekend? Elodi and her husband are setting up a stall for me to display and sell my paintings. When I told Elodi how busy you were, she offered to come and pick them up the day before. Her husband will construct the stall and deliver my work to it. I just have to get myself there before seven-thirty to set up."

"Just so long as no-one else gets murdered, there should be no problem," I reply, wryly.

"Oh, darling," she says. "Things are really bad just now, aren't they?"

I don't want to worry her at her busiest time of year, so I say, "Don't concern yourself. There's nothing I can't cope with. You just concentrate on Christmas, because before you know it, it will be upon us."

When it's time for her to head off to work, I drive her to the orchard then make my way into town to pick up my lottery ticket. Since having a significant win in the past, I buy my ticket religiously each week. I'm in the queue waiting to be served by the newsagent's son, when I see Monique standing at the side of the counter speaking to the owner.

"This letter is my formal notification, giving you one month's notice," she says. "I'm moving into my boyfriend's studio apartment which is attached to his house, so I won't need to rent from you any longer. I've been very comfortable in your apartment, but he has a lovely house with a large garden, and I'll be living there rent free."

She sees me in the queue, and smiles at me triumphantly.

"After the holidays, I'll be moving into the main house with him. We're just waiting for his wife to move out. We don't want to upset her or their children at Christmas, although the children are grown up and they'll always have a home with us. My boyfriend is going to pay for rented accommodation for his wife, so she won't be homeless."

Her voice has increased in volume, she wants everyone to hear.

"They'll be getting divorced soon, and we'll be planning a summer wedding. Do you have a copy of 'Bride' magazine? It's never too soon to get some ideas."

It's not just me who is shocked. Everyone in the shop is silenced by her revelation.

She turns. "Have you all heard enough now?" she asks, addressing the queue. "I know you've all been gossiping behind my back. Now you don't need to."

She shakes hands with the startled shopkeeper before marching out of the shop. There's a muttering of conversation as people share their opinions. This cannot be happening, I think. This must not happen.

When I step outside, Monique is there, waiting for me.

"Bonjour, Danielle, ca va?" she says, her voice sickly sweet like caramel. "Did you like my little speech? Probably not. I'm sure you hate me, but I don't care. You'll still have to be polite to me and dance to my tune, when I'm the mayor's wife, or I'll tell Francis, and he can damage you. Oh, what fun I'll have when we're married."

This is the last straw. I see the red mist descend but I'm helpless to stop it.

"You stupid, little whore," I say. "Don't you know the whole town hates you? Everyone is talking about you, and not in a good way. They laugh at your ignorance. Nobody gives a fig about Francis. Marjorie is the one who's loved. If they separate, you and your idiot, grandad lover will both be run out of town. Don't ever speak to me again. Come near me and I'll hurt you."

I hold up my hand as if I'm going to slap her. She squeals and steps backwards, away from me. Wrongfooted, she slips off the kerb and falls onto the road.

"You're in the right place now, bitch," I say. "In the gutter with the rest of the vermin."

I storm off, still livid. I know there will be repercussions from our chat, but I'm too angry to care.

I sit by the river and lose track of time, but I'm still upset. When I get back home, Patricia and Marjorie are both there. They greet me with kisses and kind words and I burst into tears.

"Oh, mon Dieu, what's wrong? Danielle, tell me, what's happened?" Patricia says.

Marjorie runs to the fridge and fetches me a glass of water. My hands are shaking so much, I nearly spill it.

"I think I'm going to need something much stronger than this," I say. "I've been really stupid. I lost my temper, and gave Monique hell. I was blazing mad. She thought I was going to slap her, and I nearly did. She fell onto the road."

"Did a car hit her?" Marjorie asks.

"No. But she grazed her elbow."

"That's a pity. I'd be happier if she'd been hit by a car," Marjorie says, smiling.

"Oh, Marjorie," I cry. "Everything's falling apart, and I can't stop it. We love you, and want to support you, but I don't know what to do."

Patricia opens a bottle of wine and we sit at the table and talk and talk. I tell them what Monique said in the newsagent's.

"The little cow!" Marjorie exclaims. "Well I'm not moving out of my house, so Francis can think again."

We've finished the first bottle of wine and have opened a second when my mobile rings. It's Francis and he's very angry.

"You'll meet me tomorrow morning at ten. I won't take no for an answer. We're going to thrash out this problem you have with Monique. I'll be waiting in the car park at the start of the walking trail, in Maurellias. It should be empty. I don't want us to be seen, for both our sakes. Be there," he orders, then ends the call.

"That was Francis. He's so angry, he could explode," I say.

"I wish he would, then my troubles would be over," Marjorie replies.

I've drunk two glasses of wine, but suddenly I don't feel like any more. Acid is burning my stomach and I feel rather sick.

"Do you mind if I leave you for a while?" I ask the girls. "I want to clear my head. I'm going to visit Poullet. I called him earlier, but he couldn't speak then. I think I'll knock on his door instead of phoning. It will be easier to talk to him face to face."

"Of course, go. We'll be fine," Patricia says, and Marjorie nods her agreement.

Soon I am driving towards my friend's house. I want to talk to him about my situation with Francis. He's lived in this town for years and understands the dynamics of it, so I know he'll give me good advice.

Chapter 25

Poullet leads me to his study and we sit facing each other on ancient, over-stuffed armchairs, the arms of which are so wide and flat, we have no need for a table to rest our brandy glasses.

"Ah, brandy, the nectar of the Gods," he says.

"My stomach feels full of acid, I'm driving, and I've already had some wine," I protest. "Do you really think I should drink this?"

"Who is the doctor here, you or me? Sip it, don't gulp it down. It's remedial. I often drive after one or two glasses of brandy. It's never done me any harm."

I think about the state of his car and smile. Every part of it is bashed. He can't park at the best of times and here he is, admitting to a cop, that he frequently drives after drinking. Being with my trusted friend, who is so kind to me, makes me emotional once again and my eyes well up.

"Sip that brandy," he commands. "I'll have no tears here. Stop feeling sorry for yourself and tell me what's troubling you."

I tell him about Monique. What she said. What I said. My conversation with Patricia and Marjorie. Francis' telephone call and his demand to meet me.

"And do you really believe Francis intends to marry this girl?" Poullet asks. "Surely not."

"I think perhaps he might." I reply, miserably.

"That wouldn't just harm you. It would hurt the whole town," he ponders. "I've never liked the man, and he has no time for me. Maybe he'll retire from office. He's served three terms, so he'd have a pension for life."

"He intends to stand for office again," I say. "And I think he'll be appointed because of all the votes he controls. Most of the municipal workers who are in the top jobs, are his friends or they're scared of him, so he'll have their votes.

And everyone who works for them as well. All the people who receive social housing benefit think he's a God – so more votes. He could be unstoppable."

"I see, I see," he replies. "No wonder you're upset. A man like him with that sort of power is dangerous, but I'm not sure what anyone can do about him."

"He wants me to meet him at ten tomorrow," I say. "He'll want me to say, yes sir, no sir, three bags full sir, and I don't know if I can."

"You will have to meet him sometime, and tomorrow is as good a time as any. Try to stay calm, no matter what he says. Don't be bullied by him, but don't antagonise him either. It will be like walking on eggshells, but you must not rise to the bait. This situation needs time to cool down. No changes will happen imminently, and we need time plan our next move. If all else fails, you have a gun," he says.

I look at him, shocked – he begins to laugh, and I laugh too. Visiting my old friend was the right thing to do. He's given me sound advice and lightened my mood.

"You're a bad old devil, Poullet," I say.

"That's why you love me," he replies.

* * *

I spend a sleepless night, tossing and turning, fearing my meeting with Francis, as I don't see how any good will come from it. I've decided not to go into the office until afterwards, so I telephone Paul and tell him he's in charge until I return.

"So," he's says, "I've to sit in your room, shout instructions and drink lots of coffee. I can do that, Boss."

"No jokes this morning, Paul. I'm not in the mood," I reply.

He can tell by my voice there's a problem, so says nothing more.

When Patricia and I sit down to breakfast, I find it difficult to make conversation. She nervously fills in the silences by prattling on about her work, the market at Ceret, Christmas dinner with my parents and Byron, anything and everything that pops into her head. Even Ollee can sense the tension in the room, and he skulks off to his bed, looking my way and whimpering occasionally, seeking approval.

"Call me when you've finished your meeting with Francis," Patricia says. "Let me know how it goes."

I nod my head. I'm too agitated to speak.

It takes me only twenty minutes to reach the car park at Maurellias. I'm five minutes early, but Francis is already there, parked under a large plane tree, near the boundary fence. As expected, nobody else is about. He sticks his hand out of the car window and beckons me over.

"Get in," he says, when I approach, and I do as he asks.

His face is strained, and he looks tired.

"Shouldn't you be resting? You're just out of hospital," I say.

"I'm well aware of that," he replies curtly. "I'm perfectly okay to talk to the likes of you."

His manner is aggressive, and I already don't like the mood he's creating.

"I'll get straight to the point, Danielle, because I don't want to waste my time with you," he begins. "You and Patricia are giving Marjorie false hope, and it has to stop. We will be getting a divorce and she will be moving out of the house before I marry Monique. I'm not a monster. I'll set Marjorie up in her own apartment and I'll pay the rent."

"Francis," I reply. "Patricia and I have had no influence over Marjorie's feelings or her actions on the matter, whatever you may think. We are her friends, and we listen to her, but we don't tell her what to do. She's an intelligent, adult woman, not some stupid little girl."

My last comment holds a barb aimed at Monique, but I can't help myself.

"About Monique," he says, "in future, when you meet her in the street you will greet her politely. Bonjour Monique, will suffice. I don't expect you two to become bosom buddies. Like me, she has an important role at the Mairie, so I suggest you don't cross her. We want no repetition of yesterday's performance."

How dare he tell me who I must be nice to. I will never speak to that woman again. I've already warned her off. Now he's pushing me too far.

"Don't you dare to tell me how I should behave," I say. "That's rich advice coming from a cheating, paedophile fornicator."

The words are no sooner out of my mouth than I regret saying them. His face turns scarlet, and he gasps with indignation.

"Monique said you were a bitch and she's right. I know how you spoke to her. She said you were trying to split us up, then you lost your temper and pushed her into the road. How could you? It's lucky she wasn't killed," he spits. "I've given you every opportunity to reassure me that you'll be sensible, but I can see my offer is wasted on you. You're obviously jealous of Monique and of our relationship."

He has worked himself into a rage. Sweat is beading on his forehead.

"Jealous of Monique?" I reply. "She's an alley cat. She'll move on to the next man as soon as you're no longer useful to her."

"How dare you," he splutters. He looks ready to explode. "I should have expected that response. You're hardly in a position to judge Monique. Look at yourself, a bitter spinster with no hope of ever getting a man; living with a dyke, and trying to pretend everything's normal. Well it's not normal. You're not normal."

I'm livid with him, and I'm about to reply, when suddenly, he clutches at his chest. His hand is frantically trying to reach into his pocket. He's looking for his spray, I think. He must be having an angina attack or another heart attack. I pat down his pockets and search for it.

He stares into my eyes, willing me to help him, unable to speak with the pain.

"Oh, you stupid man," I say. "Don't you see, you've brought this upon yourself."

He passes out. I check for a pulse, but can't find one. Then I quickly take out my phone and dial the emergency services. "Please hurry," I say. "The man is having a heart attack. There's no pulse and he's stopped breathing. I'm a police officer and I'm going to begin C.P.R."

I drag the unconscious man from the car, no easy task with a dead weight, and start to work on him. I continue trying to revive him, and feel his rib break under my hands, but no matter what I do, there's no response. I keep trying until an ambulance arrives, and the crew take over, but it's futile, I know he's dead.

I feel chilled and am unable to stop shaking. Frances went from aggressively attacking me to dead as a doorpost, in a very short time; it feels surreal. The ambulance crew try everything to revive him, but after a further fifteen minutes, they declare him dead at the scene.

A few minutes later, Paul arrives at my side. I'm so pleased to see him.

"The emergency services contacted me when they heard your name mentioned," he explains. "I've left Bernard running the office. Are you all right, Danielle?" He uses my first name because he's treating me as a victim. "What an awful thing to happen. You must be very shocked."

"I am," I say. "One minute we were chatting and the next minute he's dead. I don't know how I'll tell his wife. His children will be devastated."

"Would you like me to come with you? I can drive you, if you'd like."

"No thanks, Paul. It's kind of you to offer, but I'll pick up Patricia and take her with me. She and Marjorie are very good friends."

A member of the ambulance crew approaches. "Do you know if he had a history of heart problems?" she asks.

"Yes, he was recently released from hospital after suffering a mild heart attack. His wife said he had angina," I reply.

"Did you find any pills or spray on his person?"

"No, he seemed to be searching for something, but he didn't find it. I checked the glove box, but there was nothing inside."

She turns to Paul. "Will you be informing his next of kin," she asks.

"Yes, we'll take care of everything. All you need do, is deal with the body," he replies. "You take care of your paperwork and we'll do the rest."

Paul gives the paramedics Francis' details, then once they drive off, we too prepare to leave the scene. After checking that I feel strong enough to drive, he makes for the office. I get into my car and carefully head home. I know I must tell Marjorie what's happened as quickly as possible; a difficult task under any circumstances. Then she can decide if the news is good or bad.

Chapter 26

Francis' funeral was a quiet affair, and apart from immediate family, only Patricia and I were invited. We were not there out of respect for the deceased, but purely to support Marjorie. A memorial service was held in the church a few days later, and it was well attended. The deputy mayor stepped in to fill the post of mayor, and Monique's job was dissolved. The new man is thirty-two years old and his young wife is a notaire with super-model looks. So, he has no need for the kind of PA services Monique can offer.

All has returned to relative normal in town and I can now concentrate on solving the murders. I am still pondering on the way the victims were killed, and the elaborate scenes that were set. When it suddenly dawns on me to check something, I telephone Foret and asked him to come to the office immediately.

"Well, here I am, at your beck and call, like a pet dog," he says when he arrives.

"Please come through to my room. I have coffee ready," I reply, trying to soften his mood.

He's of no use to me if he's confrontational. I need his help not his belligerence.

When we are seated, I ask, "How many boys died at the home over the entire time it was running?"

He answers immediately, "Three," he says. "All of them in the same year. It was a dark time."

"Was there anything significant about that year? Did anything change?"

"Nothing really. Pere Gregory's work load increased. Instead of merely holding mass for the boys and listening to their confessions, he became an advisor. So, he was spending more time at the home, working with the residents. Apart from that, nothing changed."

"How did the three boys die?"

"Two committed suicide and one died of hypothermia. It was terrible, awful. Henri and I discovered Joseph Toury, dead on the mountain; he'd fallen. He'd been out there for hours, in the middle of winter. It was one of the coldest years ever recorded. When we found him, he was naked apart from one sock. The paramedics said it was common, in cases of severe hypothermia, for victims to strip off their clothes, thinking that they're too warm, when in fact, they're freezing to death. Christian Mayer hanged himself. He was a very sensitive boy, very complex, and deeply unhappy. I think his home life was troubled. He told me once that his father used to beat his mother."

He stops and sips his coffee. The Mayer family, as described by the other son, Luke, gave me a much different picture of family life before Christian's demise, but I make no comment.

"Sebastian Parc hid behind the tool shed and cut his wrists," he continues. By the time we found him, it was too late to save him. That boy was always getting into scrapes. He'd just been to the hospital the day before with a broken rib. He found it impossible to obey rules, and we weren't sure how to deal with him. I suppose we failed these young men, but we tried to turn their lives around. 'You can't win them all', as the saying goes."

And there it is, staring me in the face, three deaths, and three similar murders. So obvious when you know what to look for and ask the right questions.

Joseph Toury, fell on the mountain - discovered naked. Pere Gregory fell off a bridge – discovered naked. Henri Boudin hanged – Christian Mayer hanged. Sebastian Parc slashed his wrists – Roland Michell died of blood loss due to slashed wrists. Someone is seeking revenge for their deaths. When I find out who it is, I'll have my murderer.

Foret hasn't yet made the connection as only some of the details of the deaths were reported. Besides, he was in Spain, not France when the stories were in the newspapers, and I only released the information that I wanted the public to know.

"Do you know anything about the boys' families?" I ask. "I know about the Mayer family, but what of the others?"

"Joseph was raised by his grandfather. There were no other relatives. After Joseph died, the old man had a breakdown – he blamed himself. As far as I know, he's still in and out of hospital. Madame Parc went to live in Malawi after Sebastian died. She volunteers at an orphanage. She told me that, as she couldn't help her own child, she would try to save other people's children. It's all very sad. She still sends me a Christmas card every year with a photo of her standing amongst a group of black children. She doesn't seem to age, only the children change. She's a remarkable woman."

So, no candidate there for my killers, I think. There must be a connection somehow; I just need to discover what it is.

I let Foret leave, but warn him that I might need to call on him again. He is very subdued and makes no complaint. I think the enormity of what has occurred has just hit him. While he was in Spain, none of this affected him, he could separate himself from it, but now it is raw and real.

* * *

The next few days are unremarkable. I've emailed Gerard with an update, which he acknowledges but makes no comment. There is very little crime reported, and none of it is serious. The supermarkets are displaying chocolates and biscuits designed for Christmas, and Christmas trees and decorations are being sold at car boot sales and in gift shops. The town is calmer, now that all the tourists have gone home, and the municipal workers seem happier now that the problem of Francis and Monique has been resolved. All is well with the world, or at least my world.

When we are eating our evening meal, Patricia reminds me that the Ceret market is tomorrow and she'll need a lift.

"No problem, darling," I say. "And I've decided to take tomorrow off, so we can have lunch together after the market. I'll just stay in town and wait for you."

"Wonderful," she says. "I'll look forward to it. One of the local galleries has already reserved five of my large, winter-scene paintings, and I only had six to sell to start with, so I might nearly sell out if people buy a lot of the smaller ones as Christmas gifts."

"That's great news," I say. "Have you seen Marjorie recently?" I ask, changing the subject. "How is she getting along? Is she coping?"

"Yes, she seems to be okay. Although, she hasn't mentioned how the children are taking the loss of their father, and I don't ask. If she needs us, she'll call. She knows we're here for her. At least she no longer needs to worry about the roof over her head. And one of my customers told me that Monique is leaving town. So, Marjorie will have no fear about bumping into her at the shops."

"I'm so pleased that Elodi has arranged for your stall tomorrow, and her husband is delivering your paintings to it," I say. "With a bit of luck, we'll have a very light load coming back."

"Yes, it's very kind of them," she replies.

"Let's have some whisky after our meal," I suggest. "In the words of the song, 'it's beginning to feel a lot like Christmas', and I feel like celebrating."

"Good idea," she replies. "You seem so much happier, Danielle, now that Francis is gone. He blighted everyone's lives with his ridiculous behaviour. I'm not sorry he's gone, and yet for years we thought he was our friend. You should be able to trust your friends not to hurt you."

Chapter 27

Ollee and I go for a walk at six a.m.; it's a cool crisp morning and still dark, but the sky is clear. I'm pleased for Patricia, as by the time she has set out her paintings on the stall, the sun will be up. People like coming to the market when it's sunny and dry, and the weather can have a marked influence on sales.

When we return to the house, Patricia is ready to leave. After eating the food that she's placed in his bowl, Ollee is content to go back to his bed. He has everything he needs for his comfort, a full bowl of water and a new marrow bone to gnaw on while we're away. It really is a dog's life, I think. Mimi has also been fed, and she's happily making for the cat flap to go for an early morning prowl. Our pets have a better life than half the world's children, I think. But to Patricia, our pets are her children.

We arrive at the market and park in a good spot, close to the gallery which has reserved Patricia's paintings. Then she and I ferry them to the car, so I can deliver them for her when it opens.

"They will give you 2,500 euros, she says, 500 euros for each one. They plan to sell them for 800 euros, and asked me to charge the higher price for the large painting I have left, so as not to undercut them. I think that's fair," she says.

"I think it's marvellous that five of the six large paintings are already sold without them even making it to the stall. It means you'll have much more room to display the smaller paintings. You must be delighted," I reply.

Elodi's stall is beside Patricia's; the aroma wafting from her soaps is intoxicating, a rich, heady mixture of flower scents, rose, lily of the valley, lavender and many more. And for Christmas, she's produced star shaped soaps scented with orange, cinnamon and cherry. They are a feast for the senses. Elodi sings as she fills her counter with her produce. Patricia joins in, and within a couple of minutes, the sound of singing can be heard all over the market. Everyone is upbeat and hopeful of a good day selling their wares. I feel truly happy.

I hang around, chatting to the people I know. Then, at nine o'clock, I make my way to the gallery to deliver Patricia's work and pick up her money. She's told me the gallery owner is called Pierre and warned me that although he may seem serious, verging on grumpy, he's really a delightful man, friendly and funny, but rather shy.

When I meet him, I find everything she's said to be true. He quickly helps me to unload the car, pays me the money, then explains that he's already sold four of the five paintings on the strength of the photographs he's shown to customers.

"Your friend is a wonderful artist," he says. "Her paintings are so vibrant, full of life and colour; my customers love them. Please tell Patricia that I'll have two commissions for her in the spring, if she can fit in the work, same size paintings at same price if that's okay."

"I'll let her know," I say, and thank Pierre.

Patricia will be delighted with the news. She loves painting and it's become a very lucrative hobby.

When I leave the gallery, I make my way to the newsagent to buy a paper, then I head for the Grand Café. The sun is now up, and I intend to sit and have a coffee, read my paper and watch the world go by. As I approach I'm surprised to see Valentin Foret already seated in the sunshine. He's accompanied by a much younger man, who is presumably his partner, Eric. Foret stands when he sees me.

"Bonjour, Officer," he says. "I do believe you're stalking me. Isn't this carrying police protection a bit far? Am I expected to buy you coffee as well? Surely not?"

I am about to protest, when he slowly grins his creepy smile, and I realise he's trying to make a joke. He introduces his partner, who is so shy, he can barely look at me.

"Eric tells me I should be grateful to you. He believes you are trying to keep me alive, even though you clearly dislike me."

I stare at him, but say nothing. I don't know how to reply without stirring things up, as what he says is true, I do dislike the man.

"Would you do me the curtesy of joining us for a few minutes?" he asks. "I've been discussing these terrible crimes with Eric, and I have some thoughts which might be helpful to your investigation."

They both smile at me. Eric too has an unsettling grin. It freaks me out and I shudder, but perhaps Foret does have information. So, I agree, pull out a chair, then sit down. He waits until the waitress brings me coffee then begins.

"The three boys who died were part of a street gang. There were seven of them arrested for stealing cars and joyriding. The two older boys were the leaders of the group, but all of them had been in and out of trouble before. The older pair were jailed on this occasion, and I've no idea what became of them. The four younger boys were sent to us. Pere Gregory took a particular interest in them, he was sure they could be rehabilitated."

He stops, sips his coffee, squeezes Eric's arm and smiles at him, before continuing.

"Henri, felt they'd be better off having no family contact. He believed their families had failed them, and it would only confuse the boys to see them. He even banned written correspondence between them. Needless to say, the boys didn't agree with him."

"They must have felt very isolated," I say.

"Possibly, but Roland kept them very busy. They were always out working, for at least eight hours a day, sometimes more. He thought that if they were working then they weren't moping around or getting into trouble."

"It isn't too difficult to see why they'd be unhappy, and perhaps become depressed or hold a grudge against Pere Gregory, Henri and Roland. So, where do you fit into this scenario?" I ask.

"Nowhere, at that time I was merely the bookkeeper. I had little contact with the boys. And, as I told you before, some of the boys sought me out for comfort. They loved me. That's how I met Eric."

Eric looks adoringly at Valentin, and nods his agreement.

"That explains why you're still alive," I say. "The murderer has no hatred for you. To him, you were invisible."

"So, it seems," he says.

"Who was the fourth boy?" I ask. "Do you remember?"

"I can't remember his second name. It's difficult to remember all the boys. Obviously, the three who died stick in my mind. I think his first name was Edward or Edgar, something like that."

A chill runs down my spine.

"Could his second name have been Martinez?" I ask.

"Maybe, maybe not. I really can't remember. You should be able to check the arrest warrants for the boys, then you'll know. Surely, as an officer of the law, that won't be beyond your capabilities."

Our conversation over, I make my escape from the ghastly man. No chance of a quiet coffee and a read of my paper now, I suspect. My head is buzzing.

When the market closes, I pack the few remaining paintings in the boot of my car and take Patricia for lunch. She is upbeat, full of excitement, as she's sold most of her work.

"Three of the paintings you put in the car are also sold. One woman has bought them all. She's given me a cash deposit, but will come to the house on Monday with a cheque for the balance. That's another six hundred euros. I'm rich, your friend is a rich woman," she says, delightedly. "I'll buy you lunch; it's the least I can do after all your help."

I don't argue with her; it makes her happy to treat me. When we are seated, I tell her my news about the murders. I don't want to spoil the mood, but I cannot contain it.

"Oh, darling, how awful," she says. "Freddy and Anna will be very upset, and their friend Alain will be devastated. Eddy is his cousin."

"I haven't yet confirmed that it is Eddy," I reply. "But I'm pretty sure it is. Alain said he was in and out of trouble for joyriding and similar petty crimes. And Alain knew about at least two of the boys' deaths. I feel quite sad that I'll have to arrest Eddy, when it will clearly upset our friends, but there's nothing I can do. It's my job. Although, first I must find him."

We both feel rather low because of my revelation, so we sit quietly until we order our lunch.

"I'm having the 'dinde'," Patricia says, brightening up and changing the subject. "In England turkey is a traditional meal for Christmas lunch. So, I'm getting in the mood early."

"Well, in that case, I'm going to order the chocolate, crème brulee," I reply.

"Oh, do they also eat that in England?" she asks. "I thought it was a French dish."

"I have no idea," I reply, laughing. "I'm merely getting into the Christmas spirit, and you make me chocolate crème brulee, and I love it."

Chapter 28

On Monday morning I discuss the new lead with my team. I've had all day on Sunday to consider my options, and know now what I must do. As Alain hasn't called me with information about Eddy's whereabouts, or even a phone number for him, I must assume that he has nothing to tell me. So, I won't question him again just now.

I ask Marie-Therese to check the records and confirm that all four boys were arrested together. Then I instruct my team.

"We need the last known addresses for Eddy Martinez and his mother," I say. "We must also speak to Madame Meyer and Luke Meyer once again, in case they can give us a lead. I think Luke Meyer is our best chance, so long as he's fit enough to speak. I wouldn't be surprised if the two young men have been in touch over the years. Eddy and Christian were friends before; perhaps Luke kept in touch with Eddy after his brother died."

Within a couple of hours Marie-Therese confirms what I already suspected; the four boys were part of the same gang and were sent to the home together. She has also traced the last known address for Madame Martinez and procured a photo of Eddy.

"Good work," I say, and she smiles shyly.

I address Bernard and Cedric. "I'd like you two to go to Madame Meyer's house," I say. "Speak to her. See if she knows anything about Eddy Martinez."

I turn to Marie-Therese. "Can you please check if Luke Mayer has been released from hospital. They've never been able to hold him for long, so I suspect he'll be back on the streets again."

"Paul and I will visit the Martinez residence and attempt to speak to Eddy's mother. With a bit of luck, even if they haven't resolved their differences, she'll have some idea of where he is."

We break for coffee and await Marie-Therese's findings. It doesn't take her long to confirm that Luke Mayer has indeed been released from the hospital.

If one of you could please call me," I say to Bernard and Cedric, "and let me know if you find Luke Mayer at his mothers' house. If not, Paul and I will check the bus station after we've spoken to Madame Martinez, and see if he's hanging around there, begging."

We finish our coffee break and Bernard, Cedric, Paul and I head for the cars. I get a buzz of excitement. My case is solved. Eddy Martinez must be the murderer. There is no-one else in the frame. All I must do now is catch him. I've chosen not to report my findings to Inspector Gerard as I don't want the boys from Perpignan to take over and beat me to an arrest. I've done all the work, and I want all the credit. Even if Perpignan isn't part of my patch.

Paul and I are nearly at the address in north Perpignan that we've been given for Madame Martinez, when I receive a call from Bernard. "We're at Madame Meyers," he says.

"You must have driven like a madman to get there so quickly," I reply.

"We did drive quickly," he admits. "We put the lights and sirens on, and remember we were travelling to the south of the city, so a much shorter journey than you have to do."

"Anyway," I say. "What have you got for me?"

"Madame Meyer has let us into her house. She's drunk and aggressive and she's told us nothing. On a more positive note, we did discover Luke here. He has a small sachet of heroin, which we are holding from him. He's in a bad way. In his words, and I apologise for the bad language, 'Eddy Martinez was his brother's friend, not his. He got Christian involved with the gang. He can't stand the fucker and blames him for the destruction of his family. He hasn't seen Eddy for years and he hopes he gets ass cancer and dies.' Not very helpful, but at least you don't have to search for him. Should I return his bag of heroin? Or should I call for an ambulance now? He's going to need one or the other very shortly."

"Give him the drugs," I reply. "Why waste the hospital's resources? He'll only score again when they let him out. He's on a determined cycle of self-destruction. He's right about one thing though, if Eddy got Christian into the gang, then he did destroy their family."

Paul drives on to the Martinez home and parks outside. It's an average, modern, semi-detached villa, not remarkable, but not shabby either. When I think about the rented slum where Madame Mayer now resides with Luke, and the very small apartment where her husband lived before his accident, I can't help but feel sad about their family's destruction. They too probably lived in a nice house on a nice street like this, before Christian died and their lives fell apart.

Paul and I walk up the concrete path. The garden is neat and tidy, and I notice the windows are clean and sparkling in the sunshine. I ring the bell. The door is opened by a rather stern looking woman. Everything about her looks tight, from her perfectly groomed hair, held in a bun, with not a wisp out of place, to her closely-fitting, crisply-ironed suit. Her mouth is narrow and pursed. She eyes us up and down.

"Yes," she says, then waits, staring at me.

I introduce us, and explain that we wish to discuss Eddy.

"He's not here," she states. "We no longer speak."

"May we come in?" I ask.

"I think not," she replies. "All I can tell you about my son is that a friend of mine saw him in Argeles, singing for his supper. He spoke to Eddy, and Eddy told him that he's been moving around playing his guitar. The season is over and he's planning his final outdoor appearance at the lakeside restaurant in St Jean. I'm not sure when, but my friend offered to take me there to see him. I think it's probably this Saturday, but it makes no difference, I'm not going. I have nothing to say to my son. I don't approve of his lifestyle, never have."

What a cold woman, I think. No wonder Eddy went off the rails with a mother like her to contend with.

"Our conversation is over, Officer. Please don't come back here. I have nothing more to say."

She steps back and shuts the door leaving us standing on the doorstep.

"What a hard, cold bitch," Paul says. "That's the first time in my career that I've not been invited into a house when I've requested it. A normal house, I mean. Not the ones I must kick the door down to enter."

"Yes," I agree, "she's horrible. But at least we have a lead for Eddy now. Time for a celebratory lunch, I think. And I'm buying."

Chapter 29

I telephone the restaurant, and they tell me Eddy Martinez will be the singer on Saturday. They are holding a luncheon rather than a dinner, because it's late in the season, with the meal being served at one o'clock and the entertainment beginning at two. They're hoping the singer will encourage people to remain in their seats and purchase further drinks. Eddy is booked to entertain the crowd for two hours.

There is nothing much we can do until then, and as the office is quiet. I tell each of my officers that over the next days they can, in turn, have some extra time off. However, I do warn Bernard, Cedric and Paul that I'll need them all to work on Saturday. Marie-Therese begs to be allowed to join us.

"It will be a great opportunity for me, Boss," she says. "It's rare, if ever, that I'll have the chance to be there when a serial murderer is arrested. I'll work for nothing," she offers. "Please, please let me come along."

"You're darned right you'll work for nothing," I reply. "And you'd better not get in the way. However, I won't deny you the opportunity, so you may accompany us."

My patience is stretched to the limit – with the waiting. I am jumpy and stressed all the time, anticipating the prize at the end of the week. My team are positively twitchy. Finally, Saturday arrives, and we gather at the office.

"Well, boys and girl, this is it. We're all going to experience a career changing moment, or one of the most bitter disappointments of our working lives," I say. "Are you ready for this?"

"Ready," they reply, almost in unison.

"My plan is to let him come on to do his set, and as long as he doesn't try to bolt, we'll let him finish. Why cost the restaurant their chance of business and upset the customers? With so many people at the luncheon someone is bound to get in the way if we go storming in. We must assume he'll have some sort of weapon about his person. By being patient, there will be less risk of a member of the public being hurt. We can position ourselves at his possible exit routes, so we have them covered while he's performing, and simply close in as he starts his final song. Are you all comfortable with this plan?"

They all nod.

"Should we wear stab vests, Boss?" Marie-Therese asks.

"As I've said, there's a likelihood he'll be armed. So yes, we must be prepared for every scenario. In cities and large towns, cops nearly always wear them, and so should we. We are much too relaxed here, because serious stuff hardly ever happens, and we rarely have to attend violent situations."

She swallows hard and I can see that she's nervous. Paul aims a friendly punch at her shoulder, and she nearly jumps out of her skin.

"I could have had a knife in my hand there," he says. "Put your vest on now." She runs to fetch it.

"Good training for the kid," Paul says. "This is a day we'll all dine out on for years to come."

"If he's there," I reply.

"He'll be there, Boss," Bernard says.

"He's no reason not to be," Cedric adds.

Pep talk over, we make our way to the cars. Paul and Marie-Therese come with me and Bernard and Cedric travel together. We agree a place to meet then we all head off for the lake.

The restaurant is packed. Every seat is taken. When he sees me, the owner, Claude comes over to speak to me. I've known him for several years and I've always found him to be friendly and helpful. I have Marie-Therese with me, but the others are discreetly keeping a low profile.

"Hello, Danielle," he says. He nods an acknowledgement to Marie-Therese. "I see you have a new girl on the team. It's good that more girls are joining the force. Would you two like a coffee? I'm afraid I can't offer you a seat. As you can see we're full."

"Coffee would be great, thanks," I reply. "I heard you've got Eddy Martinez singing today. Is that why you're so busy?"

"The youngsters particularly like him. He looks like a modern-day hippy with his dreadlocks, but he's got a sweet voice and he doesn't do any loud, outrageous stuff, so he's ideal for here. Hang around for a while, he'll be on in a couple of minutes. Surely there's nothing you must rush off for. Stay and enjoy the show," he offers.

If only he knew, I think. I hate deceiving him, but needs must.

When Eddy comes on to the makeshift stage, he sits on the stool that's been placed there for him and adjusts his guitar. He looks around the room as if searching for someone. Then gives a shy smile and a wave towards a couple sitting at the front. The woman throws him a kiss, and I realise, with surprise, that it's Madame Martinez. She has come to his show, after all. The man with her must be the friend she spoke of. It's then that I realise, she's angry with Eddy, not because she hates him, but because she loves him. She wants him to have a more conventional lifestyle, one she understands.

He looks around again. Our eyes meet. He holds up his hands in a placatory fashion and nods. He knew we'd be here. His mother must have told him we were searching for him. He seems resigned to it. Eddy begins singing. He does indeed have a sweet voice. We wait. When he is about to start his final number, he gives me a sign as if asking whether he should come to me or will I come to him. He obviously has no intention of making a run for it. I sign back, that I'll come to him, and Marie-Therese and I make our way forward. As does Paul. When his song ends we move in.

"Hello, officers, I've been expecting you. My mother telephoned me," he says. "May I pack up my guitar and get my pay, before we leave?"

I realise then that Madame Martinez is at my side.

"May I kiss my son?" she asks. Then she steps forward and hugs him before I can answer. "Go with the police, son," she says. "I'll collect your money from Claude for you. He knows me well, so there'll be no problem. It will be waiting for you when you return."

"Thanks, Mama, but you keep the money, I won't be back for a long time," he replies.

I would find the situation very poignant if my heart wasn't racing with joy. I have him. I have the murderer, and this will make me famous on a national scale.

Bernard and Cedric walk over to us. They are the ones who discreetly take Eddy to their car.

"See you at the shop," Bernard calls to me, as he helps Eddy into the back seat.

Once they drive off, Paul puts his arms around Marie-Therese and me and he hugs us.

"I feel a promotion coming on," he says. "And more money, and fame. The newspapers will love this face," he says, stroking his chin. "Who wouldn't love this face?"

"Everyone except your mother," Marie-Therese quips.

Our mood is light. We can't help grinning because we are so pleased with ourselves. The arrest was easy; he gave himself up, but still, we'll be heroes.

As we drive back to the office, I think about all the people who'll be happy and relieved the case is solved. Poullet will have answers for his wife, Foret will no longer be at risk, Inspector Gerard can once again do little, but gain a lot of kudos, and as for Junot – well he'll have the scoop of a lifetime.

When we get to the office we sit down at a desk with Eddy on one side and Paul and I on the other. Bernard, Cedric and Marie-Therese keep a discreet distance away, but nobody wants to go home. Bernard quickly runs to the baker and picks up a large bag of croissants while Marie-Therese makes coffee. Then we are ready to begin the interview. I formally charge Eddy with the three murders and offer to get him a solicitor. He declines.

"I'm guilty," he says. "I killed them all. They had to die, and they had to know why they were being put to death."

He is emotionless, cold.

"Why don't you tell us, in your own words, what this is all about. Why kill them after all these years?" I ask.

Tears start to flow down his cheeks. His hands shake as he lifts the coffee cup to his lips.

"They killed all my friends and destroyed their families. Their regime was too harsh; they tortured us. Sebastian couldn't take any more, he slashed his wrists. It was Roland Michell who drove him to it. Sebastian lost all hope. His mother lives in Africa. She couldn't even bear to remain in France after he died."

A sob escapes from his throat; he pauses for a moment, swallows hard, then continues. "Joseph was so badly beaten by Pere Gregory, that his ribs were broken. The man was a sadistic monster. He was always picking on Joseph. He said he'd beat the devil out of him. Joseph tried to run away. He fell on the mountain and froze to death."

His voice is breaking, he inhales deeply, then releases his bated breath before continuing.

"Christian was my best friend. He was so full of despair he hanged himself. That was due to Henri Boudin – he drove him to take his own life. He was a teenage boy, just a child really, and he hanged himself. Can you imagine how desperate he must have been?"

He pauses to take a handkerchief from his pocket, dries his eyes and loudly blows his nose.

I give him a moment to compose himself then say, "I realise how awful your lives were, it must have been hell. But why now after all this time? Why kill them now?"

"I met Luke Mayer begging at the bus station a few months ago. He was distraught. His father, Charles, had just driven his car into a wall, trying to end his life, because he couldn't live with the guilt any longer. He couldn't save Christian and he blamed himself. He'd been struggling with his mental health for years, ever since Christian died. Luke's mother is a hopeless drunk and Luke is a junkie. The whole family were destroyed because of these monstrous men. Something in me just snapped. I had to get rid of them. I had to kill them to avenge my friends. They were vermin and vermin must be wiped out."

And there it is, the answer I've been looking for. I now have a motive for the killings as well as a confession. I feel exhausted. I could lay my head on the desk and sleep, but instead I call Gerard's mobile and fill him in on what's happened. He's delighted, and keeps thanking me for my 'sterling work', as he puts it.

Within the hour, cops from Perpignan arrive to take Eddy away and we are free to leave.

Chapter 30

There is chaos in town when the story breaks. Once again, a media circus arrives, but we don't mind this time as the news is all good. Paul gets his wish and is interviewed, not only by a national newspaper, but by a local tv station as well. He is ecstatic. He also manages to be a guest on local radio.

"I'm in the wrong job," he states. "The public love me, the media loves me, I could be a star."

We all roar with laughter. "Any particular star?" Marie-Therese asks. "Or will any burnt out old sun do?"

I like that girl; she has the ability of bringing a person down to earth with one line. I offer her a permanent post to begin when her training finishes, and I'm delighted when she accepts. She could have her pick of practically any station after her involvement in the murder cases, but she likes it here.

"Better being a big fish in a small pond, than a small fish in a big one," she says, and I'm inclined to agree with her. Besides, she'll earn the same pay, wherever she works, but here she'll essentially be doing a PR job, and she'll be an individual instead of simply a number. One day I can see this girl filling my shoes, but not for some time yet, I hope.

Junot hugs me every time he sees me in the street, but worse than that, he declares to anyone who'll listen, 'I love this woman, she's amazing'. I try to discourage him, but he can't seem to help himself. His most recent scoop has won him a permanent job with a national newspaper. He'll be moving to Paris in a couple of weeks. At least then, the hugging will stop. It's embarrassing, and people are beginning to talk. I constantly tell them that there's nothing going on between us, God forbid!

There's a very good chance that Eddy Martinez will end up in a hospital rather than prison. His lawyer is pleading insanity as his defence. It's clear he's been terribly damaged by being in the home, so, he might be successful.

Madame Poullet baked me a cake to thank me for solving the case and finding Saint Henri's killer. It was enormous – enough for every member of staff and their families to have some. No wonder the good doctor is the size of a baby elephant. Still, it was kind of her to show her appreciation. She's recommended me and my staff for an award, and the new mayor will be only too happy to oblige. He loves his position and credits me with making his job simpler.

Marjorie's children were understandably extremely upset at the death of their father, but they were already used to him not being in their lives very often, so they haven't missed him as much as one might have expected.

It's now the start of December and soon the spa will close for the winter, and the last of the 'curists' will go home. Everyone is looking forward to the holidays. The story about the murders is now yesterday's news. Even the most spectacular crimes are nine-day wonders, and now the newspapers are full of feel good sagas and seasonal adverts.

Patricia and I are having lunch seated at the kitchen table. She is excitedly telling me about her plans for Christmas dinner.

"I hope you don't mind," she says, "but as well as your mama and papa and Byron, I've also invited Marjorie. Her children are visiting their grandparents for the holidays. They were all invited, and she didn't want to deny Francis' family access to the kids, but she couldn't face going to their house. It's too soon. She still feels bad about how Francis treated her before he died."

"Of course, she must come to us," I reply. "We're her friends and we'll always support her, besides, she's good company."

"Marjorie says that her life is much calmer now that Francis has gone. He was very difficult to live with. However, she's pleased you were with him at the end. She's happy that he wasn't alone. I'm sure you did everything to save him."

I look at her sweet, trusting face, and I know I must tell her more about that day.

"There's something I have to tell you, darling," I begin. "I hope you'll understand."

She stares into my eyes and smiles. "This sounds serious," she says.

"It is," I reply. "Frances and I were arguing. I was very angry with him because of the way he was treating Marjorie. He was going to divorce her, marry

Monique and force Marjorie out of the family home. She would have lost everything: her husband, her home, and she'd have been financially ruined, relying on Francis and Monique for every little thing. I couldn't bear it."

"No wonder you were arguing with him," she says. "Do you think the fight caused his heart attack?"

"I'm sure of it," I reply. "I feel so guilty."

"You have nothing to feel guilty about. You were only trying to protect our friend. He was the one causing all the problems. If the C.P.R. had worked, you would have saved him."

"If I'd found his medicinal spray, I might have saved him," I say.

"But he didn't have it with him. The hospital told Marjorie that. You checked his pockets and there wasn't one."

"I hope you can forgive me, Patricia, but I didn't tell you the whole truth. After I tried and failed to revive him I found his spray in the glove box of the car. I didn't want Marjorie to know I'd missed it, so I threw it away. If I'd found it sooner, things might have been different."

She stands, comes to my side of the table and puts her arms around my shoulders. "Please don't be upset, Danielle," she says. "You did everything possible, given the circumstances. He was a horrible man who pretended to be our friend. Marjorie is safe now, and none of us will miss him. Put all the bad thoughts out of your mind. It will soon be Christmas, and it's time to move on."

It feels good to unburden myself. Patricia has forgiven me for my shortcomings, and nobody else needs to know this truth.

Chapter 31

ANOTHER TRUTH

I'm pleased I told Patricia my story. Confession is good for the soul, even a dressed-up confession, like mine. However, there are some facts that are undeniable. I did argue with Francis, it did cause his heart attack, and I'm very happy that he's dead. Although, perhaps one or two things are not quite as clear as I portrayed them.

We bend the rules, tell white lies, speak the truth, but not the whole truth; if the outcome is good, what does it matter?

It all began when I went to visit Poullet. We were discussing the problems that Francis was causing, and he made a joke. 'If all else fails, you have a gun', he said. This conversation led to further talk about methods of death. Morbid, perhaps, but cops and doctors go hand in hand with death.

"Do you know that a person can die from an air embolism?" he said. "No poison, no bullets, a simple injection of air into an artery can kill you. In someone with a heart problem, it might leave no trace. The perfect murder, perhaps."

"An injection with a syringe, like one used to draw blood?" I asked.

"No, no, that wouldn't do. You'd need one like this," he said, lifting a box of syringes from a drawer. "It would have to be filled with air then injected into an artery, say in the neck, and for good measure, more than once."

"So, a person, would have to fill the syringe with air, inject it into an artery, then do the same thing a couple of times again, to be sure of killing someone?" I reply. "I assume they'd have to be incapacitated first for it to work, otherwise they'd fight back, surely?"

"Never having tried it myself, I'm not sure," he admits. "But I did once see someone die from an air embolism when I was a young doctor. It was very quick and lethal. There was no way to revive the patient. The brain stopped, and she died, end of story."

When Poullet left the room to fetch some biscuits, I slipped one of the syringes into my handbag. I didn't have a concrete plan at that time, but I wanted to give myself options. Did Poullet expect me to take one? Did he think I might have to use it? Possibly – probably. We've both had to make life or death decisions before, and we understand each other.

I met Francis in the car park as arranged. He made me so angry with his comments that I wanted to hurt him; I wanted him dead. I goaded him and pushed him until he clutched at his chest. He was having a severe angina attack.

"You stupid man," I said. "You've brought this upon yourself."

He frantically searched for his medication spray, but in his panic, he'd forgotten that he'd placed it in the glove box of his car. I patted down his pockets and, thinking I was trying to help him, he stared gratefully into my eyes, before he passed out from the pain. He didn't realise that I was making sure that if it was in his pocket, I'd get to it first.

My hands shook as I filled the syringe with air. I had trouble injecting it into the artery in his neck because my hand was so unsteady. The second and third time were easier, and I managed to place the needle into the exact same spot.

Poullet was right, he died very quickly.

I dragged his body from the car, no easy task, phoned the emergency services then began C.P.R. making sure I broke his rib in the process. I didn't want them to think my attempts to revive him were half-hearted. When they arrived, I returned to his car and that's when I came across his spray in the glove box. No need for anyone to know it was there, I thought. So, I placed it in my pocket then I locked up his car. On my way home, I threw it from my open car window, over the side of the mountain. But no-one need know that either.

It's only one week until Christmas. When I walk through the streets of my small town, people greet me and give me gifts. I'm everybody's friend. This town is a safer and better place with me in it. I am the person everyone turns to in a crisis. It gets me thinking. The deputy mayor is very pleasant, but he's not strong. He likes to go with the flow, and he hates confrontation. He's a nice man, but nobody really likes nice. A good mayor must also be tough, and when required, be ruthless.

The mayoral elections are next year, and whilst I like my job, do I really want to do this much work as I grow older? Everyone is always saying that they'd like someone like me to be the mayor. So why not me? It would be an easy life: attending openings of events, going to meetings about ordinary things, shaking people's hands and being praised, simply for being the mayor. I'd know everything that's going on and be in control. I'd work much fewer hours and have free meals and coffee in the local restaurants and bars. I'd probably get more pay, and I wouldn't have to answer to selfish idiots like Inspector Gerard. It would be so much easier than sitting in my stuffy room each day. The mayor's office has the latest air conditioning and a super-duper coffee machine, and the official car is top of the range. I could do the job with my eyes shut.

So why not me?

End

A Message from Danielle

Thank you for reading Hanging About in the Pyrenees, I do hope you enjoyed it. If you've read the first five books in the 'Death in the Pyrenees' series, you will know the journey I've travelled to reach this stage and what a journey it has been. However, if you've had no previous knowledge of my life and would and would like to catch up with my ups and downs and highs and lows, you can meet my friends and colleagues and some of the less desirable individuals who have lived, and died, here - available now the first five books. You may also like to read other books written by Elly Grant and all of them are listed below.

Other books by Elly Grant

Palm Trees in the Pyrenees
Take one rookie female cop
Add a dash or two of mysterious death
And a heap of prejudice and suspicion
Place all in a small French spa town
And stir well
Turn up the heat
And simmer until thoroughly cooked
The result will be surprising

Palm Trees in the Pyrenees is the first book in the series 'Death in the Pyrenees.' It gives you an insight into the workings and atmosphere of small town France against a background of gender, sexual, racial and religious prejudice.

The story unfolds, told by Danielle a single, downtrodden, thirty-year-old, who is the only cop in the small Pyrenean town. She feels unappreciated and unnoticed, having been passed over for promotion in favour of her male colleagues working in the region. But everything is about to change. The sudden and mysterious death of a much hated, locally-based Englishman will have far reaching affects.

Grass Grows in the Pyrenees
Take one female cop and
Add a dash of power
Throw in a dangerous gangster
Some violent men
And a whole bunch of cannabis
Sprinkle around a small French spa town
And mix thoroughly

Cook on a hot grill until the truth is revealed

Grass Grows in the Pyrenees, second book in the series "Death in the Pyrenees," gives an insight into the workings and atmosphere of a small French town and the surrounding mountains, in the Eastern Pyrenees.

The story unfolds told by Danielle, a single, thirty-year-old, recently promoted cop. The sudden and mysterious death of a local farmer suspected of growing cannabis, opens a 'Pandora's' box of trouble. It's a race against time to stop the gangsters before the town, and everyone in it, is damaged beyond repair.

Red Light in the Pyrenees
Take one respected female cop
Add two or three drops of violent death
Some ladies of the night
And a bucket full of blood
Place all in, and around, a small French spa town
Stir constantly with money and greed
Until all becomes clear
The result will be very satisfying

Red light in the Pyrenees, third in the series Death in the Pyrenees, gives you an insight into the workings and atmosphere of a small French town in the Eastern Pyrenees. The story unfolds, told by Danielle, a single, thirty-something, female cop. The sudden and violent death of a local Madam brings fear to her working girls and unsettles the town. But doesn't every cloud have a silver lining? Danielle follows the twists and turns of events until a surprising truth is revealed. Hold your breath, it's a bumpy ride.

Dead End in the Pyrenees
Take a highly-respected female cop
Add a bunch of greedy people
And place all in a small French town
Throw in a large helping of opportunity, lies and deceit
Add a pinch in prejudice
A twist of resentment
And dot with death and despair.

Be prepared for some shocking revelations
Dangerous predators are everywhere
Then sit down, relax and enjoy
With a dash or two of humour
And plenty of curiosity

Dead End in the Pyrenees' is the fourth book in Elly Grant's 'Death in the Pyrenees' series. Follow Danielle, a female cop located in a small town on the French side of the Pyrenees as she tries to solve a murder at the local spa. This story is about life in a small French town, local events, colourful characters, prejudice and of course death.

Deadly Degrees in the Pyrenees

The ghastly murder of a local estate agent reveals unscrupulous business deals which have the whole town talking. Michelle Moliner was not liked, but why would someone want to kill her? The story unfolds, told by Danielle, a single, thirty-something, female cop based in a small French town in the Eastern Pyrenees. Danielle's friends may be in danger and she must discover who the killer is before anyone else is harmed.

Deadly Degrees in the Pyrenees is the 5th book in the Death in the Pyrenees series. It's about life, local events, colourful characters, prejudice and of course death in a small French town.

The Unravelling of Thomas Malone

The mutilated corpse of a young prostitute is discovered in a squalid apartment.

Angela Murphy has recently started working as a detective on the mean streets of Glasgow. Just days into the job she's called to attend this grisly murder. She is shocked by the horror of the scene. It's a ghastly sight of blood and despair.

To her boss, Frank Martin, there's something horribly familiar about the scene.

Is this the work of a copycat killer?

Will he strike again?

With limited resources and practically no experience, Angela is desperate to prove herself.

But is her enthusiasm sufficient?

Can she succeed before the killer strikes again?

and here's the first few pages to sample -

Prologue

Thomas Malone remembered very clearly the first time he heard the voice. He was twelve years, five months and three days old. He knew that for a fact because it was January 15th, the same day his mother died.

Thomas lived with his mother Clare in the south side of Glasgow. Their home was a main door apartment in a Victorian terrace. The area had never been grand, but in its time, it housed many incomers to the city. First the Irish, then Jews escaping from Eastern Europe, Italians, Polish, Greeks, Pakistanis, they'd all lived there and built communities. Many of these families became the backbone of Glasgow society. However, situations changed and governments came and went and now the same terraces were the dumping ground for economic migrants who had no intention of working legally, but sought an easy existence within the soft welfare state system.

A large number of the properties were in the hands of unscrupulous landlords who were only interested in making money. They didn't care who they housed as long as the rent was paid. So as well as the people fleecing the system, there were also the vulnerable who they exploited. Drug addicts, alcoholics, prostitutes, young single mothers with no support, they were easy pickings for the gangsters. The whole area and the people living within it smacked of decay. It had become a no-go district for decent folk, but to Thomas Malone, it was simply home.

Thomas and his mother moved to their apartment on Westmoreland Street when Clare fell out with her parents. The truth was they really didn't want their wayward daughter living with them anymore. They were embarrassed by her friends and hated their drinking and loud music. When Clare became pregnant, it was the last straw. Thomas's grandparents were honest, hard-working, middle-class people who had two other children living at home to consider. So when Clare stormed out one day after yet another row with her mother, they let her go. She waited in a hostel for homeless women for three weeks, before she realised they weren't coming to fetch her home and that's when Clare finally grew up and took charge of her life in the only way she knew how.

When Thomas walked home from school along Westmoreland Street, he didn't see that the building's façades were weather worn and blackened with grime from traffic fumes. To outsiders they looked shabby and were reminiscent of a mouth full of rotting teeth, but to Thomas they were familiar and comforting. He didn't notice the litter strewn on the road, the odd discarded shoe, rags snagged on railings, or graffiti declaring 'Joe's a wanker' or 'Mags a slag'. He functioned, each day like the one before, never asking for anything because there was never any money to spare.

He was used to the many 'uncles' who visited his mother. Some were kind to him and gave him money to go to the cinema, but many were drunken and violent. Thomas knew to keep away from them. Sometimes he slept on the stairs in the close rather than in his bed so he could avoid any conflict. He kept a blanket and a cushion in a cardboard box by the door for such occasions. Many a time, when he returned from school, he found his mother with her face battered and bruised, crying because the latest 'uncle' had left, never to return. It was far from being an ideal life, but it was all he knew so he had no other expectations.

It was a very cold day, and as he hurried home from school, Thomas's breath froze in great puffs in front of him. He was a skinny boy, small for his age with pixie features common to children of alcoholics. His school shirt and thin blazer did little to keep him warm and he rubbed his bare hands together in an attempt to stop them from hurting. He was glad his school bag was a rucksack because he could sling it over his shoulder to protect his back from the icy wind. As his home drew near his fast walk became a jog, then a run, his lungs were sore from inhaling the cold air, but he didn't care, he would soon be indoors. He would soon be able to open and heat a tin of soup for his dinner and it would fill him up and warm him through. He hoped his mother had remembered to buy some bread to dunk.

As Thomas approached the front door something didn't seem right, he could see that it was slightly ajar and the door was usually kept locked. There was a shoe shaped imprint on the front step, it was red and sticky and Thomas thought it might be blood. There was a red smear on the cream paint of the door frame, which he was sure was blood. Thomas pushed the door and it opened with a creak; there were more bloody prints in the hallway.

Thomas took in a great breath and held it as he made his way down the hall towards the kitchen. He could hear the radio playing softly. Someone was singing 'When I fall in love'. He could smell his mother's perfume – it was strong as if the whole bottle had been spilled. The kitchen looked like a bomb

153

had hit it. His mother wasn't much of a housekeeper and the house was usually untidy, but not like this. There was broken crockery and glassware everywhere and the radio, which was plugged in, was hanging by its wire from the socket on the wall, dangling down in front of the kitchen base unit. A large knife was sticking up from the table where it was embedded in the wood. The floor was sticky with blood, a great pool of it spread from the sink to the door, and in the middle of the pool lay the body of Thomas's mother. She was on her side with one arm outstretched, as if she were trying to reach for the door. Her lips were twisted into a grimace, her eyes were wide open and her throat was sliced with a jagged cut from ear-to-ear. Clare's long brown hair was stuck to her head and to the floor with blood and her cotton housecoat was parted slightly to expose one, blood-smeared breast.

Thomas felt his skinny legs give from under him; he sank to his knees and his mother's blood smeared his trousers and shoes. He could hear a terrible sound filling the room, a guttural, animal keening which reached a crescendo in a shrieking howl. Over and over the noise came, filling his ears and his mind with terror. Then he heard the voice in his head.

"It's all right, Son," it said. *"Everything will be all right. I'm with you now and I'll help you."*

He felt strong arms lift him from the floor and a policeman wrapped him in a blanket.

"Don't be frightened," the voice told him. *"Just go with the policeman. Someone else will sort out this mess. It's not your problem. Forget about it."*

"Thank you," he mouthed, but no sound came out.

The policeman gathered Thomas in his arms and carried him from the room. It was the last time he ever saw his mother and he cannot remember now how she looked before she was murdered. The voice in his head, the voice that helped him then, remains with him today guiding and instructing him; often bullying, it rules his every thought. Sometimes, Thomas gets angry with it, but he always obeys it.

The Coming of the Lord

Breaking the Thomas Malone case was an achievement but nothing could prepare DC Angela Murphy or her colleagues for the challenge ahead.

Escaped psychopathic sociopath John Baptiste is big, powerful and totally out of control. Guided by his perverse religious interpretation of morality, he wreaks havoc.

An under-resourced police department struggles to cope, not only with this new threat, but also the ruthless antics of ganglord, Jackie McGeachy.

Pressure mounts along with the body count.

Glasgow has never felt more dangerous.

Never Ever Leave Me

'Never Ever Leave Me' is a modern christmas romance

Katy Bradley had a perfect life, or so she thought. Perfect husband, perfect job and a perfect home until one day, one awful day when everything fell apart.

Full of fear and dread, Katy had no choice but to run, but would her split-second decision carry her forward to safety or back to the depths of despair? A chance encounter with a handsome stranger gives her hope.

Never ever leave me, sees Katy trapped between two worlds, her future and her past. Will she have the strength to survive? Will she ever find happiness again?

Death at Presley Park

In the center of a leafy suburb, everyone is having fun until the unthinkable happens. The man walks into the middle of the picnic ground seemingly unnoticed and without warning, opens fire indiscriminately into the startled crowd. People collapse, wounded, and dying. Those who can, flee for their lives.

Who is this madman and why is he here? And when stakes are high, who will become a hero and who will abandon their friends?

Elly Grant's 'Death At Presley Park' is a convincing psychological thriller.

But Billy Can't Fly

At over six feet tall, blonde and blue-eyed, Billy looks like an Adonis, but he is simple minded, not the full shilling, one slice less than a sandwich, not quite right in the head. When you meet him, you might not notice at first, but after a couple of minutes it becomes apparent. The lights are on but nobody's home. In Billy's mind, he's Superman, a righter of wrongs, a saver of souls and that's where it all goes wrong. He interacts with the people he meets at a bus stop; Jez, a rich public schoolboy; Melanie, the office slut; Bella Worthington, the leader of the local W.I. and David, a gay, Jewish teacher. This book moves along quickly as each character tells their part of the tale. Billy's story is darkly funny, poignant, and tragic. Full of stereotypical prejudices, it offends on every level, but is difficult to put down.

Released by Elly Grant Together with Zach Abrams

Twists and Turns

With fear, horror, death and despair, these stories will surprise you, scare you and occasionally make you smile. *Twists and Turns* offer the reader thought provoking tales. Whether you have a minute to spare or an hour or more, open *Twists and Turns* for a world full of mystery, murder, revenge and intrigue. A unique collaboration from the authors Elly Grant and Zach Abrams

Here's the index of Twists and Turns -

Table of Contents

A selection of stories by Elly Grant and Zach Abrams ranging in length across flash fiction (under 250 words), short (under 1000 words) medium (under 5000 words) and long (approx. 16,000 words)

- Time to Kill (medium) by Elly Grant

- Fight (flash) by Zach Abrams

- Just Desserts (medium) by Elly Grant

- Interruption (flash) by Zach Abrams

- I've Got Your Number (medium) by Elly Grant

- Rhetoric (flash) by Zach Abrams

- Keep It to Yourself (medium) by Zach Abrams

- Lost, Never to be Found] (medium) by Zach Abrams

- Man of Principal] (flash) by Zach Abrams

- Witness After the Fact] (medium) by Zach Abrams

- Overheated] (flash) by Zach Abrams

- Wedded Blitz] (medium) by Elly Grant

- Taken Care] (flash) by Zach Abrams

- The Others] (short) by Elly Grant

- Waiting for Martha] (long) by Elly Grant

and here's the first few pages to sample -

Waiting for Martha

The 'whoooo aaaaah' accompanied by blood curdling shrieks sent the Campbell brothers screaming down the path. They tore along the street without a backward glance. Martha Davis and her three companions doubled up with laughter. They were all dressed as zombies and, to the naïve eyes of primary school-aged children, they were the real thing.

"Did you see the middle one move?" Alan Edwards asked. "He could be a candidate for the Olympics. He easily left his big brother behind."

"That's because the older one's a lard ass," John Collins replied unkindly. "His bum cheeks wobbled like a jelly. Fat kids shouldn't wear lycra. If the real Superman was that chunky he'd never get off the ground."

"The middle one overtook him because he was trying to help the younger one and was holding his hand," Martha observed. "I'm sure that little fellow pee-ed his pants, he was terrified. He's only about five."

"Yeah, great, isn't it?" Fiona Bell added laughing. "I love Halloween, don't you?" she said clapping her gloved hands together with pleasure.

The teenagers had hidden around the corner of Alan's house to jump out at unsuspecting children who came trick or treating. They were all aged fifteen except for John Collins whose birthday had been in June, he was sixteen but looked older. He was a big lad, tall and broad with an athletic build, he looked like a grown-up where the others still looked like children. Fiona Bell was nearly sixteen her birthday was on the fifth of November, Guy Fawkes night, so the group would be celebrating next week with fireworks. She was the spitting image of her mother being of medium height with long blonde hair and a heart shaped pretty face. Alan Edwards's birthday was in January. He was short with straggly black hair and he was a bit of a joker. Martha Davis, the baby of the group, was born in March and was a willowy looking beauty with Titian coloured hair. They were in the same class at school and had a reputation for being cool and edgy. None of them was ever actually caught for their various misdemeanours, but they were often seen running away from trouble. Being teenagers they thought they knew it all and, smoking, drinking, wearing only black and never telling their parents anything, was par for the course. Living in a village meant they didn't have easy access to drugs but the friends made roll-ups using everything from dried orange peel to crushed tree bark and convinced each other it had some psychedelic effect. They'd all been born in the village and had been friends since playgroup. They trusted one another with their worries and secrets and their friendships endured through petty squabbles and jealousies. Although unrelated, they were like a family.

By seven o'clock the procession of 'victims' had all but dried up – the word had got out, it seemed – so Martha and her friends decided to change venue.

"Time to go to church," Alan suggested. "If we hide just inside the gates of the churchyard, we'll get them as they walk by."

"That's a great idea," John added. "They'll think we've risen out of one of the churchyard graves. We'll scare the shit out of the little darlings."

"You lot go ahead and I'll catch you up. I'm going home for a warmer sweater and a quick bite to eat. I've not had my dinner yet and I'm starving. I'll just be about half an hour," Martha assured.

"Why didn't you grab something to eat before you came out? The rest of us did. Now you'll miss out on some of the fun," Fiona said, sounding disappointed. Martha was her best girl friend and she didn't want to be stuck on her own with the two boys. They could get incredibly silly without Martha. She was the mother figure of the group and she always managed to stop them from going too far.

"Don't worry Fiona, I'll not be long, and you two," she said pointing to the boys, "Behave yourselves."

"Yes Mom," they replied in unison, hanging their heads and pulling comical faces.

"See what I have to put up with when you're not there, anyone would think they were two years old."

Martha stared at her three friends, her face had a serious expression and for a moment it looked as if she might cry. "I love you guys," she said. "I'll be as quick as I can."

"Are you okay?" Fiona asked. "You look a bit upset."

"I'm fine, really fine. My eyes are just watering with the cold. It's freezing out here."

Martha gave each of them a hug and off she raced towards her home. The others quickly made their way to the church and positioned themselves behind one of the large wrought iron gates. The gates hadn't been closed for over fifty years and ivy grew thickly round them affording the teenagers cover. For the next forty minutes, they had a ball scaring adults and children alike until one of their teachers, Mr. Johnston, came along. As the three friends jumped out shrieking, he clutched his heart and fell to the ground. They thought they'd killed him. They were kneeling on the ground beside him each trying to decide how to do CPR when he suddenly sat up and shouted "Got ya!" The tables were well and truly turned and they nearly jumped out of their skins.

"It's not so funny when you're on the receiving end, is it?" he said rising to his feet. "Haven't you got homes to go to? And where's the fourth one? Where's your friend, Martha?"

"She went home for some food," Fiona said. "She should have been back by now."

"I think you should all run along and find her. You've done enough damage here for one night."

Mr. Johnston brushed himself down and walked away. After their shock, the three friends had indeed had enough.

"Martha should have been here ages ago," Alan said. "I'm getting cold now. Let's go to her house and see what's keeping her."

"Good idea," John agreed.

"But what if she's on her way and we miss her?" Fiona protested.

"Come on," Alan said, pulling her arm. "I'm not waiting any longer and you can't stay here on your own. A real zombie might leap out of a grave and get you. If Martha arrives and we're gone, she'll go home and she'll find us there."

"I suppose you're right," Fiona conceded.

"I'm always right," Alan said smugly. "Come on, let's get going before my ears fall off with the cold."

The three friends headed along the street towards Martha's home. They were damp and tired and they hoped that Helen Davis, Martha's mum, had hot soup for them. She always had soup on the stove in winter and she fed the three of them as if they were her family.

"I hope Mrs. Davis has pumpkin soup, it's my favourite," John said,

"Yeah, the chilli she puts in it really gives it a kick," Alan agreed.

"Aren't either of you just a teensie bit worried about Martha? She's been gone for over an hour now and she's never usually late," Fiona said. "Get a move on you two, I want to make sure she's all right."

When they reached Martha's house and rang the bell they were surprised when her Dad, Michael, answered instead of her.

"Well, well, what have we here?" he asked, laughing at their attire. "Is Martha hiding? Where is she?"

"She left us over an hour ago, to come home for some food," Fiona said. "We thought she was still here. When did she leave the house?"

"Martha hasn't been home," her father replied. "If this is some sort of Halloween joke, it's not funny." He stared at the teenagers. "The jokes over – where's Martha?"

A chill ran through each of the friends and Fiona's eyes welled with tears. "We don't know," she said helplessly. "If she didn't come home then she's been gone for over an hour. Something might have happened to her, maybe she's fallen. We'd better go back and look for her."

"Wait for me. I'm coming with you," Mr. Davis replied. "I'll just go and tell Martha's Mum what's happening."

After a couple of minutes Michael Davis returned and Helen was with him. When she saw the state Fiona was in, Helen put her arm around the crying girl's shoulders and tried to reassure her, "Don't worry, pet, we'll find her," she said. "She won't have gone far. She probably stopped to chat to someone and lost track of the time."

"We'll split into three groups," Michael Davis said. "Alan and John, you take the street leading to the church. Helen and Fiona, you walk towards the primary school and I'll take the road that goes around the outside of the village. We'll meet back here in half an hour. No, better make it forty-five minutes," he said looking at his watch.

The boys looked uncomfortably at Fiona, they would have much rather stayed together but they had no choice. Mr. Davis had taken control, and as he was an adult and a teacher, they felt they should do what he said. Besides, the sooner they found Martha the sooner they could go home.

They searched the whole village knocking on several doors as they went. The group met up after the arranged forty-five minutes then searched again. By ten o'clock, there was nowhere left to look for her. The next day was a school day and the three teenagers had now reached their curfew, but they were reluctant to go home with Martha still missing. Michael Davis was grim faced. Helen was beginning to panic.

About the Author

Hi, my name is Elly Grant and I like to kill people. I use a variety of methods. Some I drop from a great height, others I drown, but I've nothing against suffocation, poisoning or simply battering a person to death. As long as it grabs my reader's attention, I'm satisfied.

I've written several novels and short stories. My first novel, 'Palm Trees in the Pyrenees' is set in a small town in France. It along with many of my other novels are published by Creativia.

As I live in a small French town in the Eastern Pyrenees, I get inspiration from the way of life and the colourful characters I come across. I don't have to search very hard to find things to write about and living in the most prolific wine producing region in France makes the task so much more delightful.

When I first arrived in this region I was lulled by the gentle pace of life, the friendliness of the people and the simple charm of the place. But dig below the surface and, like people and places the world over, the truth begins to emerge. Petty squabbles, prejudice, jealousy and greed are all there waiting to be discovered. Oh, and what joy in that discovery. So, as I sit in a café, or stroll by the riverside, or walk high into the mountains in the sunshine I greet everyone I meet with a smile and a 'Bonjour' and, being a friendly place, they return the greeting. I people watch as I sip my wine or when I go to buy my baguette. I discover quirkiness and quaintness around every corner. I try to imagine whether the subjects of my scrutiny are nice or nasty and, once I've decided, some of those unsuspecting people, a very select few, I kill.

Perhaps you will visit my town one day. Perhaps you will sit near me in a café or return my smile as I walk past you in the street. Perhaps you will hold my interest for a while, and maybe, just maybe, you will be my next victim. But don't concern yourself too much, because, at least for the time being, I always manage to confine my murderous ways to paper.

Read books from the 'Death in the Pyrenees' series; enter my small French town and meet some of the people who live there – and die there.

To contact the author ellygrant@authorway.net

To purchase books by Elly Grant link to http://author.to/ellygrant

Lightning Source UK Ltd.
Milton Keynes UK
UKHW042112230221
379286UK00008B/365/J

9 781034 475675